"IT'S A MIRACLE. . . ."

"The sun will show its face again. . . ." *"The sight of the seers will be restored. . . ."* *"The Chosen One alone will suffer as she has never suffered."*

Sarah stopped reading for a moment, frowning. *That makes two of us.* Who *was* the Chosen One, anyway? Was she even a person, a human being?

Whoever she was, she seemed to have a lot in common with Sarah—like the way they had both lost their brothers at the end of January. It was strange. Sarah leaned forward and kept reading. There was some stuff about the Demon, and then: *"In a final hour of need, the Chosen One will be saved."*

Lucky for her, Sarah thought grimly. Well. If the coincidences kept up, maybe Sarah would be saved, too. Yeah, right. And maybe she'd wake up and find out the melting plague was just a bad dream.

Finally, at the bottom of the page, there was another one of those sequences of three numbers ending in ninety-nine: *"Arbah ehhad tisheem veteyshah."*

A date, obviously. 4/1/99. *Hold on.* That was today, wasn't it?

"Sarah! Sarah, come here! It's a miracle!"

Sarah's head jerked up. Ibrahim was staggering down from the ridge, maniacally waving his arms.

"There's a boat!" he cried. He stopped and thrust a hand out toward the sea, jumping up and down like a jack-in-the-box. "We're saved! There's a boat!"

About the Author

Daniel Parker is the author of over twenty books for children and young adults. He lives in New York City with his wife, a dog, and a psychotic cat named Bootsie. He is a Leo. When he isn't writing, he is tirelessly traveling the world on a doomed mission to achieve rock-and-roll stardom. As of this date, his musical credits include the composition of bluegrass sound-track numbers for the film *The Grave* (starring a bloated Anthony Michael Hall) and a brief stint performing live rap music to baffled Filipino audiences in Hong Kong. Mr. Parker once worked in a cheese shop. He was fired.

COUNT DOWN

APRIL

by
Daniel Parker

Simon & Schuster
www.simonsays.com/countdown/

First Aladdin Paperbacks edition March 1999

Produced by 17th Street Productions,
a division of Daniel Weiss Associates, Inc.
33 West 17th Street, New York, NY 10011

Aladdin Paperbacks
An imprint of Simon & Schuster
Children's Publishing Division
1230 Avenue of the Americas
New York, NY 10020

Cover design by Mike Rivilis
The text of this book was set in 10.5 point Rotis Serif.
Printed and bound in the United States of America
10 9 8 7 6 5 4 3 2 1

Library of Congress Cataloging-in-Publication Data
Parker, Daniel, 1970–
April / by Daniel Parker. — 1st Aladdin Paperbacks ed.
p.   cm. — (Countdown ; 4)
Summary: After everyone on Earth over twenty dies, the awakened Demon called Lilith continues to spread her influence, while the teenagers chosen to stop her hope to unleash the power of an ancient encoded scroll.
ISBN 0-689-81822-X
[1. Supernatural—Fiction.] I. Title. II. Series: Parker, Daniel, 1970-   Countdown ; 4.
PZ7.P2243Ap   1999
[Fic]—dc21   98-50564
CIP   AC

To Beth and Andy

APRIL

The Ancient Scroll of the Scribes:

In the fourth lunar cycle,
During the months of Nisan and Iyar
in the year 5759,
The sun will show its face again.
A blanket of living things
will cover the land.
And the sight of the Seers
will be restored.
But a false prophet
will arise in the New World,
Aided and empowered by the
servants of the Demon,
Deceiving the Seers with illusions
of magic and healing powers.
The Chosen One alone will suffer
as she has never suffered.
Death will court her—
tempting her with its dark sleep.
While the Demon assumes a human form,
walking among the righteous and the wicked.
Seen but not seen. Heard but not heard.
Her name will be sealed
within a name, as the dark
secrets are sealed within this scroll.
The servants of the Demon
will prepare the land.
And in a final hour of need,
the Chosen One will be saved.

Fearing a rotten end, scaring a pig with songs,
the evil eye brings the terror
to the red box and atlas.
Four one ninety-nine.

The countdown has started . . .

The long sleep is over.

For three thousand years I have patiently watched and waited. The Prophecies foretold the day when the sun would reach out and touch the earth—when my slumber would end, when my ancient weapon would breathe, when my dormant glory would blaze once more upon the planet and its people.

That day has arrived.

But there can be no triumph without a battle. Every civilization tells the same story. Good requires evil; redemption requires sin. The legends are as varied as are the civilizations that spawned them— yet each contains that same nugget of truth.

So I am not alone. The Chosen One awaits me. The flare opened the inner eyes of the Visionaries, those who can join the Chosen One to prevent my reign. But in order for them to defeat me, they must first make sense of their visions.

For you see, every vision is a piece of a puzzle, a puzzle that will eventually form a picture . . . a picture that I will shatter into a billion pieces and reshape in the image of my choosing.

I am prepared. My servants knew of this day. They made the necessary preparations to confuse the Visionaries—all in anticipation of that glorious time when the countdown ends and my ancient weapon ushers in the New Era.

My servants unleashed the plague that reduced the earth's population to a scattered horde of frightened adolescents. None of these children know how or why their elders and youngers perished.

And that was only the beginning.

My servants have descended upon the chaos. They will subvert the Prophecies in order to convert the masses into unknowing slaves. They will hunt down the Visionaries, one by one, until all are dead. They will eliminate the descendants of the Scribes so that none of the Visionaries will learn of the scroll. The hidden codes shall remain hidden. Terrible calamities and natural disasters will wreak havoc upon the earth. Even the Chosen One will be helpless against me.

I *will* triumph.

PART 1:

April 1, 1999

Citicorp Building,
Seattle, Washington
9:30 A.M.

"Go! . . . Go! . . . Go! . . ."

I really can't deal with the college-frat-party vibe,
Ariel Collins thought dizzily. True, she was lying on
her back with a rubber hose rammed into her mouth,
gulping beer as fast as she could. But how could she
be expected to maintain control with all this stupid
yelling? For one thing, she was profoundly wasted.
For another, she was about to start cracking up. And
an attack of the giggles would *not* be in her best in-
terest right now. No.

"Whatever you do, Ariel, don't laugh."

Oh, crap—

All at once her throat caught, and the expanding
mass of fizzy warmth seemed to surge back through
her gullet. The next thing she knew, she was shriek-
ing with laughter and spewing beer all over herself.

"Loser!" the chorus of voices hooted at once.

All right. Enough was enough. She had to regain
some semblance of dignity. She rolled over on the
dingy red carpet and struggled to sit up straight. Her
eyes were stinging—but she didn't know if that was
because of the beer or the morning sun. It was *way* too

5

bright in this lobby. A tangle of stringy, beer-soaked, brownish blond hair flopped in front of her face.

"You can't *do* that, Caleb!" she cried. She coughed a few times between giggles. "There's beer coming out of my *nose!*"

Caleb Walker stood directly over her, clutching the hose with his right hand. He rubbed his left hand on the one ratty T-shirt he possessed: a black rag that drooped from his beanpole frame like a wilted leaf.

"Do what?" he asked. He flashed an innocent grin. "Beer's good for your nose. Good for your hair, too. We're out of shampoo, remember?"

She tried to scowl at him, but she ended up giggling again. It was crazy: Just *looking* at Caleb was enough to make her laugh. She could honestly stare at that goofy smile and those bright blue eyes for hours. And the amazing thing was that he seemed to get better looking with each passing day. He'd lost a lot of weight—they all had—but his sinewy slimness, was, well . . . kind of sexy. Especially with that wild mane of long brown hair. Not that she would ever tell him or anything, obviously.

Caleb cocked an eyebrow. "Anyway, since when do *you* make the rules?"

"In case you forgot, *chump,* I'm the one who constructed this magnificent funnel. Therefore I alone am responsible for any rules regarding its use."

She *was* pleased with it, actually—in spite of the sarcasm. For the first time ever, she'd created something with her own hands. On a whim she'd found an old funnel and a six-foot length of hose and fastened them together all by herself. From scratch, no less.

Trevor (may he rot in hell) would have been proud. He was always so cocky about being the one family member with any talent for building and fixing things. As if reading military engineering textbooks instead of having friends was something to be proud of.

Of course, the main reason she'd made the funnel in the first place was to *forget* about her twisted brother. And to forget about her father's gruesome death and the past in general . . . and mostly to forget how her onetime boyfriend, Brian Landau, had split town and was probably never coming back. She figured the faster the alcohol entered her system, the quicker she'd be able to block out reality.

"Sure, you *built* it," Caleb stated smugly. "But face it, Ariel. Out of all of us, you're the only one who can't even *use* it."

"Oh, yeah?" She racked her brain for a witty comeback, but the fog of booze and sleep deprivation left her mouth hanging open like an idiot. It was pitiful. They all needed some sleep. *Badly*. She glanced around at the rest of the drunken posse, the same bedraggled group who'd been living in this abandoned lobby for almost two months—Marianne, Jared, Cynthia, and John. The four of them were starting to look like clones: a quartet of haggard faces, dirty hair, bloodshot eyes, and shaky smiles that lingered for way too long. . . .

"Want to give it another shot?" Caleb asked, eyeing the funnel seductively.

Ariel shook her head. "I think I'm gonna crash," she mumbled. She pushed herself to her feet and squinted toward the huge glass windows. *Jesus*. She had to find an area of carpet that was out of the light, away from the stink of all the empty beers.

"But you *can't* crash," John protested. He opened a fresh bottle. Then he grabbed the funnel from Caleb and began pouring beer into it—spilling a froth of amber liquid onto the floor. Ariel rolled her eyes. Even when John *hadn't* been drinking for seventy-two hours straight, his mind wasn't exactly razor sharp. Luckily Caleb snagged the hose and plugged the end of it with his thumb.

"Why can't I crash, John?" she asked dryly.

"It's my birthday," he said.

Ariel smirked. "Your birthday was two days ago."

A semideranged grin formed on his lips. "I know. But I haven't slept. The party's still raging. And it's still the same party. So, *technically,* it's still my birthday, right?"

"Right." Ariel blinked a few times. "Yeah. Mm-hmm. You know, now I understand what Caleb was talking about."

John's eyes narrowed. "What's that?"

"I was explaining why you repeated the fourth grade three times," Caleb replied. "See, you *think* differently from the rest of us, John."

"Or you don't think at all," Ariel added with a grin.

John shrugged. He was smiling now, too. "Just in case you forgot, I *am* the only high-school graduate among you lowlifes. And being as school's out forever and none of you are ever gonna get a diploma, that means none of you are ever gonna achieve the level of wisdom that I . . ." He left the sentence hanging.

"What was that, wise man?" Caleb teased.

But John just shook his head.

Ariel stared at him, frowning. He really *was* plastered, wasn't he? He started swaying—then abruptly dropped the funnel, spilling beer all over himself. The bottle slipped from his fingers and splashed to a puddle on the carpet at his feet.

"Whoa, there, buddy!" Caleb cried.

John lurched forward. He wasn't smiling anymore.

Wait a second. Ariel looked at him closely. Something was wrong with him. His face was turning red. His eyes were bulging. There was a gurgling noise in his throat. . . .

Oh, my God. Ariel clamped her hands over her mouth. *It's happening!*

A black mark crept out from under John's T-shirt and up onto his Adam's apple.

"John?" Caleb asked.

There was no answer. In a matter of seconds the blackness spread from John's neck to the rest of his body, darkening his face and hands and arms.

His flesh started bubbling.

No, no, no. Ariel tried to step back, but her joints seemed to lock and freeze. She was unable to do anything but gape at him.

Blood spurted from his mouth.

"John!" Cynthia screamed. "John!"

It was too late. His body was already crumpling in on itself, melting away like snow in a fire, dripping into nothingness. . . .

And then he was gone.

Only his clothes remained, lying in a puddle of

black slime that mixed with the beer and blood on the carpet.

Ariel's eyes flashed to Caleb.

Caleb was staring at the liquid remains, shaking his head, his face a mask of terror and disbelief. "This isn't right," he gasped tremulously. "He's not old enough. He's only nineteen. He—he just turned nineteen. . . ."

Nobody said a word. Ariel's head spun. She couldn't comprehend what had just happened; it had been too quick, too unreal. Caleb was right. John *shouldn't* have died. The melting plague only struck people over twenty and under sixteen. They'd all seen enough death to know that; they'd witnessed dozens of meltings right here in this very lobby. Was the plague getting stronger? After all, nobody had any idea how it worked. Maybe it was somehow closing in on—

"He lied," Jared breathed.

Ariel tore her gaze from the puddle. "What?"

Jared nodded. His face had turned a chalky white. The color stood out in stark contrast to his scruffy brown whiskers. "He lied. It was his twenty-first birthday."

"His twenty-first?" Caleb whispered.

Marianne suddenly burst into tears. *"Why?"* she wailed.

Jared lifted his shoulders slightly. "He . . . uh, I don't know. I didn't want to ask him about it. I guess I was the only one who knew."

"No, I thought he was older, too," Cynthia remarked in a toneless voice. "You know the joke around school. People were always ragging on him, saying they had to let him graduate before he hit retirement age."

"It makes sense," Ariel found herself saying.

"What does?" Jared demanded.

"I mean, just that . . ." She bit her lip, then turned her attention back to the carpet. "He must have known he was going to die. That's probably why he didn't want to go to sleep. That's probably why he didn't want to stop partying. It's like . . . you guys know him better than I did, but I bet he wanted to go out with a bang and not freak everyone out. And who knows? Maybe he told the lie enough times that he started to believe it himself." Nobody replied.

Once again the bottle-strewn lobby was perfectly silent.

Ariel's gaze flickered across each troubled face. She took a deep breath. Were they thinking the same thing she was? Were they wrestling with the same feelings? Were they mad at John for lying? And were they relieved at the same time? Ariel couldn't deny it; she was thankful that John *wasn't* nineteen. As harsh as that seemed, it meant that *she* had a few more years. The plague remained at a distance, somewhere off in the future.

"You know what it's time to do," she said.

The five of them glanced at one another.

Without a word they drew together in a circle around the remnants of John's body.

"John Currin was our friend," Ariel whispered.

"John Currin was our friend," the others repeated in unison.

She looked at Jared. "You start," she murmured.

Jared nodded, swallowing. He bent over and plucked one of John's socks from the muck.

11

"One of, uh . . . one of the things I liked best about John was the way he could talk his way out of anything," he said. "I'm going to keep this sock to remind me of John."

"John Currin was our friend," everyone chanted a second time.

There was a pause. Ariel nodded to Cynthia.

Cynthia sniffed. She hesitated, then reached over and carefully extracted his dripping watch, using just the tips of her thumb and forefinger. "I . . . well, I liked a lot of things about John. But, um, I guess the thing I liked the most was the way he was never on time." She forced a laugh, but her voice caught in her throat. "I—I'm going to keep this watch to remind me of John," she finished.

"John Currin was our friend," the group chanted again.

A tear fell from Ariel's cheek. It was strange: In the past she'd always avoided events like this. She wasn't religious or anything. She'd always weaseled her way out of going to church. All the formalized prayers and songs and rituals made her feel weird, like she was putting on an act. But in the face of the plague she desperately needed *something*, some kind of ceremony—some way to mark the passing of each new victim . . . so that none of the dead would ever truly be gone. Every single one would stay alive in the memories of those who remained, until the very last person on earth vaporized.

It had nothing to do with church or God or the devil. It had to do with people. With human beings. With *kids*. It had to do with taking just a minute to remember in the middle of trying so hard to forget. . . .

"Caleb," Ariel whispered. "Your turn."

Caleb cleared his throat.

"I . . . I . . . ," he stammered.

Ariel held her breath. Caleb wiped his eyes. His hands were trembling violently. He took a step forward, then froze.

"Go on," Ariel encouraged, as gently as she could.

But Caleb remained still.

"What is it?" she asked. "What did you like best about John?"

He simply shook his head. Then he turned and sprinted out the door, vanishing into the morning sunshine.

The Fourth Lunar Cycle

Naamah understood the power of fire.

All of the Lilum had a special, intimate relationship with things that burned. The lighting of a candle marked the beginning of every rite, every invocation, every offering to the Demon. Fire was Lilith's essence. Fire was Lilith's right hand. But among the mortal and earthbound, Naamah alone appreciated the terrible magic of it—on a deeper level than anyone could possibly imagine.

She alone witnessed the explosion that decimated the Aswan High Dam.

She alone saw how the flames turned the once mighty structure into a pathetic heap of impotent rubble. She alone saw how the flames burst forth and multiplied with every breath of air, how they were alive but not alive. . . .

And so she had a new appreciation for the task demanded of the fourth lunar cycle. But that was the subtle majesty of Lilith. Every success brought a new insight, a new revelation.

Naamah drew in a deep breath, surveying the torch-bearing Lilum as they scurried about the woods and lit the assembled piles of kindling. Until now she had never seen the sun-dappled forests of America, never witnessed the first bloom of spring in such a crisp and unspoiled wilderness. It was really quite beautiful. Only the rustling of black robes disturbed the tranquility . . . until the crackle of flames grew to a roar.

The time had come.

"Dark is she, but brilliant!" Naamah cried.

"Black are her wings," the rest of the Lilum answered as one. "Black on black!"

"Her lips are red as roses, kissing all of the universe!" Naamah continued.

And the Lilum answered, "She is Lilith, who leadeth man to ruin!"

Billowing smoke and flame began to obscure the trees. Naamah smiled. Soon this place would be an inferno, and no one would pass. Across the globe the Seers would be drawn—

There was a tap on her shoulder.

"Our work is done," a familiar voice whispered. "The helicopter is ready."

Naamah turned around.

Ah, yes . . . Amanda. The priestess from Ohio. The one who'd picked this place and gathered the necessary tools. They'd met for the first time at dawn, but Naamah already knew much about her. She knew that Amanda's coven had singlehandedly lured over a hundred Seers to their deaths. An impressive number. But then, Naamah also knew that two of those Seers had escaped Amanda's clutches: a boy and a girl. It was Naamah's business to know the secrets of all the Lilum. They were all sisters in the same cause.

Amanda bowed subserviently. Waist-length black hair tumbled out from under her hood and shrouded her eyes.

"You may rise," Naamah said.

The girl stood and quickly led Naamah away from the flames—through the trees to a nearby pasture, where the helicopter waited, blades whirling.

Naamah paused at the edge of the forest. "You've done well here," she stated.

Amanda lowered her eyes. "Thank you. But I . . ." She left the sentence unfinished.

"I know what you're thinking," Naamah soothed. "Don't worry about the boy and the girl. They're just children. Two frightened and confused children. Believe me, Amanda. They'll both come back to us soon enough."

Highway 64,
Lexington, Nebraska
11:35 A.M.

George Porter was never the type of guy to count his blessings. He never had any blessings to count. But at this particular moment he was feeling pretty damn lucky.

I got a lot to be grateful for, don't I?

First off, he was grateful that he'd found this black Volkswagen Bug at the edge of Lake Shelbyville. He'd hit the jackpot. It was practically brand-new. It drove like a dream. It had a half-full tank of gas, too. That was a freaking miracle. And, of course, he was grateful that he'd been blessed with the skills to bust into any car at any time—and start it without any keys.

Most of all, however, he was grateful that he'd learned how to swim at the Churchill Juvenile Detention Camp for Boys.

Yup. He never thought that he'd have a reason to thank the Pittsburgh Police Department for anything—but then again, he'd seen enough weird crap in the past three months to know that fate worked in mysterious ways. If those cops hadn't been such hard-asses about his mastering the breaststroke last

19

summer, he would have drowned for sure when the lake flooded. So he owed The Man big time because now he found himself cruising westward down a tree-lined highway with a beautiful girl asleep in the seat next to him. Make that a beautiful *woman*. It was pretty hard to imagine that the two of them almost died in a flash flood only a week ago.

How the hell had he even *survived?*

Oh, well. There was no point dwelling on the past. He felt kind of sick even thinking about it. Besides, a lot of things in his life were harder to believe than escaping that flood. Like the way Julia Morrison, the best-looking and coolest girl he'd ever met, was now his girlfriend. Or like the way every single adult who'd ever been a jerk to him was now just another black stain on the pavement. Well, actually . . . no, that was easy to believe. After all, he kept bouncing over old clothes and avoiding car wrecks—

"Stop it!" Julia shrieked.

George jerked in his seat.

He hadn't said all that stuff out loud, had he? He shot a quick glance at her, his heart pounding. But she was clearly asleep—squirming in the passenger seat, her eyes closed, her dark curls falling over her delicate brown skin. She must have been having some kind of nightmare.

"Julia?" he asked anxiously, his eyes flashing between the road and her face.

She didn't respond. Her face was all sweaty. She looked as if she were in pain.

"Julia, wake up! Wake up!"

Her eyes remained closed.

"The Demon," she moaned. "The Demon is near. Have to . . . have to stop it."

A vision. She's having a vision. George swallowed, unsure of what to do. Should he stop the car? No, no—standing still made him anxious. He *had* to keep moving. Ever since the flood he'd gotten that *feeling* again, that tug toward the west. . . . It haunted him now worse than ever. Julia felt it, too. Besides, she'd had visions while driving before. She'd just never spoken out loud like that—

"The Demon!" she yelled. "The Demon is coming. George!"

"Shhh," he whispered shakily. He struggled to concentrate on the road. A truck seemed to pop out of nowhere. *Dammit!* He spun the wheel, narrowly whizzing past it, then shot a glance at the rearview mirror—catching a quick glimpse of his own frightened green eyes and messy blond bangs. The car swerved back across the dividing lines. He suddenly felt as if the forest on either side were closing in on him.

"It's gonna be all right, Julia. Just hang on. . . ."

"Why don't you run?"

Run? What was she *talking* about? He shook his head, gripping the wheel with both hands. Things were all messed up. Julia's visions shouldn't last this long. Something wasn't right. She should be snapping out of it—

Oh, no.

There was a hiss in his ears.

A rushing noise.

Have to stop the car, he thought.

All at once he had a massive head rush . . . *vroom,* like jumping over a ramp on a skateboard. Okay. He couldn't panic. He knew what he had to do. There wasn't much time. He tried to hit the brakes, but his leg wouldn't budge. His foot felt as if it were caught in quicksand. Darkness crept up on him, closing the doors on his sense of sight. He was barely conscious of the highway rushing past the windows.

"Julia," he croaked. "Julia, help me. . . ."

The ocean glistens in the moonlight.
It's so beautiful and peaceful—like glass.
The night is very still. I can hear the waves lapping softly against the base of the cliff.
But there's fear in the air, too. Why?
My baby is crying. Her eyes are filled with tears. I look at them: one green, one brown. And then I understand. I know the Demon is near. It's closer than it's ever been . . . but I can't see it. I can hear it laughing at me. The laughter comes from all around, from every direction. Why won't it show its face?

"Come out!" I shout at it. "Come out and show yourself!"

"George—can you hear me?"

George's eyes popped open. *Whoa.* At first he was too disoriented to comprehend what he was seeing. It was just . . . a white wall, lit up with a weird kind of red glow. His neck felt strained and out of joint. And there was something pressing down on his lap—

"Wake up!" Julia shouted. "Please!"

His head snapped down. The realization came to

him: He'd passed out, and his head had fallen back. He'd been staring at the ceiling of the car. Julia was climbing over him, fighting to hit the brakes and control the wheel. And as for the glow . . . it was coming from the huge and rapidly approaching fire burning directly in front of them, maybe a quarter mile up the highway.

"Crap!" he yelled. "Julia—"

The car squealed to a stop.

George jerked forward, pushing Julia against steering wheel. "Ow!" she cried.

He struggled to lean back. "Sorry, sorry . . ."

She squirmed out from under him and flopped back into her seat.

"Are you all right?" he gasped. For some reason, he was shivering. Maybe it was because he still had no idea what was going on. His heart bounced painfully in his chest. One second he was driving, the next Julia was screaming, the next he was having a vision, now . . .

"Fine," she breathed. "How about you?"

He just shook his head. His eyes wandered back to the fire.

Damn. The whole *forest* was lit. A raging wall of flame stretched as far as he could see, pumping an evil black cloud toward the sky. Funny. He didn't feel so lucky or grateful anymore. Nope. He felt as if he might puke.

"What happened?" he whispered. "Where did this come from?"

Julia bit her lip. "I don't know," she answered. "I woke up, and you were passed out. You must have been having a vision. I grabbed the steering wheel. That's when I saw the fire."

He turned to her, staring into her soft and fearful brown eyes for what seemed like a long time. How long had he been out? A minute? Ten minutes?

"Well . . . um . . . what do you think we should do?" he finally asked.

She shook her head. "I don't think there's anything we *can* do. We have to turn around."

"But that . . ." He swallowed. "That means going east. Not west."

"I know, George," she said quietly. "I know."

THREE

**An island in the Red Sea,
near the Egyptian Coast
4:45 P.M.**

The sun was killing Sarah Levy.

She knew it. Slowly but surely, she was dying. She crouched in the dust under the wreckage of the camel-drawn carriage, desperately trying to hide from the blinding glare . . . but it was useless. Most of the carriage's canvas roof had collapsed. It lay among the ripped Persian tapestries and splinters of wood—right beside the stinking carcass of the dead camel. The back end was the only part of the carriage that remained standing. And at its skewed angle it created only a tiny patch of shade, hardly big enough to shield a child. Some of the hideous red blisters on her burned arms and legs had already burst—

"I am going to devote my life to Satan!" a hysterical voice shouted.

Sarah closed her eyes. *Ignore him,* she repeated to herself. *Ignore him.* . . .

But five full days had already passed, and the mantra was wearing thin.

She tried to lick her cracked lips. Her dry tongue lay trembling in her mouth like a bloated fish out of water. *Water.* She shook her head. Her throat involuntarily

25

struggled to swallow. It was stupid to think about water; she *knew* that. She knew all about thirst. After all, she'd been caught out in the Sahara Desert once . . . but, of course, that thirst was nothing compared to what she felt now. This thirst was like a physical *presence,* a living *thing*—robbing her of her strength, strangling her. How many days had she gone without a drop? Three?

"Sarah, did you hear me? Allah does not exist! Satan is my ruler!"

"Be quiet," she croaked. She wasn't sure whom she hated more: Ibrahim Al-Saif, the religious fanatic who claimed to be in love with her—or Ibrahim Al-Saif, the lunatic who ranted nonstop about Satan. At least when he'd kept her captive, he'd been *calm.* He'd been *lucid.* But ever since that freak earthquake had created this God-forsaken desert island, he'd gone totally insane.

"Sarah!"

Uneven footsteps shuffled toward her.

Oh, no. Sarah raised her head and squinted across the shimmering, rocky wasteland. Ibrahim was fast approaching, teetering unsteadily on bare feet. *Good God.* He was barely recognizable—naked from the waist up, his white pants torn and soiled, his lean brown torso soaked in sweat. Even through her fogged glasses she could tell that his eyes had lost their sparkle. They looked like two broken bits of dull black clay. Did *she* look as frightening?

"I am going to take my own life," he wheezed.

She simply stared at him. What did he expect her to say to that?

"Do you hear me?" he demanded. "I am going to throw myself into the sea! I am going to swim westward until I die. I must go west! Satan commands it!"

"Look, you haven't eaten or drunk anything in three days," Sarah mumbled. She ran a shaky hand through her damp brown hair. "You're just going through—"

"I have nothing to live for!" he shouted. His voice cracked. "If I go west, then—"

"Will you please *shut up?*" she barked. She tore her glasses off her face and wiped the lenses on her sweat-drenched T-shirt—mostly to do something, *anything*, besides look at Ibrahim. "I don't want to hear it."

He didn't say anything for a moment. Then he collapsed to his knees and buried his face in his hands. "I . . . I'm so sorry," he choked out. He began to sob quietly. "I don't know what's happening to me. . . ."

Sure, you do, she thought, putting her glasses back on. *You're losing your mind.*

"What about the scroll?" he cried. He lifted his head and stared at her with a look of crazed urgency. "You said it had powers. You said that it—"

"Ibrahim, we talked about this," she interrupted. "Remember? I looked at the scroll. There's nothing in it that can help us. *Nothing.* All right?"

He blinked a few times. His jaw hung slack, as if he didn't understand. "What about the code? You know . . . that code you kept talking about?"

"Do *you* want to find the code?" She whirled around and thrust her hands under a filthy tapestry,

27

where the ancient parchment lay hidden from the sun. With a grunt she grabbed the two wooden pegs and yanked them free, then shoved the scroll in Ibrahim's face. The violent movement kicked up a cloud of dust. "Here!" she yelled. "Go ahead!"

He recoiled from her, coughing. "How can I find it?" he whimpered. "I don't read—"

"You don't read Hebrew," she finished flatly. "Yes, Ibrahim. I know. So it looks like we're back to square one. Which is nowhere."

"But why won't you just try again?" he pleaded. "Please. You said you cracked the first part of it. You said it told you when the rain would end, and you were right. Maybe if you look one more time . . ."

Sarah glared at him. The more Ibrahim talked, the more tense and irate she became. He was sapping her strength. At this point he was practically draining the life out of her. She had to shut him up, make him go away—any way she could.

"Listen, I'll read it on one condition," she muttered after a few seconds. "You leave me alone and don't say a word."

A brief smile appeared on his trembling lips. Then he pushed himself to his feet and scampered up to the crest of the ridge, slumping into the dust to face the vast blue sea.

Sarah shook her head.

He's lost it. He's totally lost it.

With an exhausted sigh she spread the delicate parchment out on the ground and began turning the creaky pegs counterclockwise, unraveling the familiar sea of tightly packed letters.

A curious nausea gripped her stomach.

Why did she agree to do this? Why was she torturing herself? She *hated* looking at the scroll. Not because she didn't believe in the prophecies. No, she hated looking at it precisely because she believed in them so *much*. She hated this scroll because she knew that every prophecy inscribed with the three-thousand-year-old black ink would come true. And unless she sprouted wings, there was no way she could warn people . . . no way at all. What did Ibrahim expect, anyway?

Well, at least he was leaving her alone. That was enough for now. She kept her eyes focused on the Hebrew months listed near the top of each block of text: Shevat and Adar . . . Adar and Nisan . . . then she stopped turning the pegs. There: Nisan and Iyar. She'd reached the part about the fourth lunar cycle—meaning the month of April. Once again she could read about bizarre and cataclysmic events that would occur while she sat here and died of thirst. Wonderful.

Her eyes wandered down the passage.

"The sun will show its face again. . . ." "The sight of the Seers will be restored. . . ." "The Chosen One alone will suffer as she has never suffered."

Sarah hesitated for a moment, frowning. *That makes two of us.*

Who *was* the Chosen One, anyway? Was she even a person, a human being?

Well, whoever she was, she seemed to have a lot in common with Sarah—like the way they had both lost their brothers at the end of January. It was strange. Sarah leaned forward and kept reading.

There was some stuff about the Demon, and then: *"In a final hour of need, the Chosen One will be saved."*

Lucky for her, Sarah thought grimly. Well. If the coincidences kept up, maybe Sarah would be saved, too. Yeah, right. And maybe she'd wake up and find out the melting plague was just a bad dream.

Finally, at the bottom of the page, there was another one of those sequences of three numbers ending in ninety-nine: *"Arbah ehhad tisheem veteyshah."*

A date, obviously. 4/1/99.

Hold on. That was today, wasn't it? The earthquake struck five days ago, so—

"Sarah! Sarah, come here! It's a miracle!"

Sarah's head jerked up.

Ibrahim was staggering down from the ridge, maniacally waving his arms.

"There's a boat!" he cried. He stopped and thrust a hand out toward the sea, jumping up and down like a jack-in-the-box. "Come look! There's a boat!"

Uh-oh. He'd finally gone over the edge. He was hallucinating.

"Come *here!*"

Summoning what little strength still remained, she crawled out into the hot sun. She was going to punch him in the face. Yes. The time had come to knock him out cold and put him out of his misery. The rays beat down upon her, slowing her every step—but she was determined to do this. She forced herself up to the ridge. . . .

"Oh, my God!" she screamed.

There *was* a boat! *Holy—*

Not just a boat. An ocean liner. A huge, white cruise ship with multiple decks.

Sarah's pulse doubled. She blinked several times. She had to make sure it wasn't a mirage, that she wasn't seeing things. But no. The vision remained. The ship was there, all right, maybe three miles to the north—drifting westward across the placid blue waters.

"We have to . . . have to signal it," Ibrahim stuttered. "We need to reflect the sun with something. We need glass, a mirror of some kind."

Sarah nodded. Her eyes darted back to the wrecked carriage. But there was no glass, only cloth and wood—

"What can we do?" Ibrahim cried.

"Fire," she murmured frantically. Yes. Fire would attract the ship's attention. They could burn the carriage. Everything was bone dry. It would be easy to light . . . only they had no lighter, no matches, nothing.

Ibrahim chewed his lip for a second. "I think I can do it," he mumbled. He bolted over to the wreckage and pulled two jagged pieces of broken support beams from the pile, then began feverishly rubbing them together.

Sarah's heart squeezed. *Oh, no.* He really *had* gone nuts. That kind of thing only worked in cartoons, for God's sake. Her eyes flashed back to the ship. It was moving slowly but steadily. In another five minutes, she figured it would be completely out of their sight.

"Your glasses!" he shouted. "Bring them here!"

My glasses? She spun around. "What—"

"Do it!" he snapped.

Her body seemed to obey his command before she could even think. She sprinted over to him and yanked her glasses off her face.

"Hold them up to the sun," he instructed. "Aim the light where the pieces of wood are touching."

Aim the light . . . But there was no time to second-guess him. She lifted her glasses to the sky. Two bright, shaky, circular spots appeared on one of the pieces of wood. She tried to keep them fixed on the exact place where the pieces rubbed against each other, but it was a battle; she was trembling too much. She overshot one way, then another—

"Keep still," he grunted.

Sarah held her breath. She had to relax. She had to forget her hunger and thirst and fear. Ibrahim's movements grew more jerky, more intense. . . .

A thin wisp of smoke rose from one of the spots of light.

Sarah's eyes grew wide. The spot quickly blackened.

"It's working!" she whispered. "It's working!"

All at once a tiny red flame leaped from the wood. Ibrahim carefully bent down and held the stick under a shred of tapestry that dangled from the fallen roof. Almost instantaneously the flame grew and began to eat its way up the cloth.

Sarah wiped her brow. Adrenaline coursed through her body. Ibrahim snatched another scrap of wood and stuck the end of it into the flames, then darted around the carriage—using the makeshift torch to light different areas.

32

Several small fires began to burn. Grayish smoke flowed into the sky.

"Blow on the flames!" Ibrahim shouted. "Blow! Fan them!"

Clenching her fists, Sarah sucked in a huge breath of hot, dry air. But when she tried to exhale, she ended up gasping and nearly falling on her face. She had no strength.

A long, low horn blast sounded in the distance.

"They see us!" Ibrahim cried. "They see us!"

She whirled, standing on her tiptoes, craning her neck to peer over the ridge.

Could it be? Yes. The ship had stopped dead in the water. A light at the tip of the bow was flashing toward them: *blink-blink . . . blink-blink . . . blink-blink . . .*

Ibrahim was right. He was *right!*

Sarah turned to him. She found she couldn't speak. A rush of emotion, too powerful to even name, had robbed her of her voice. Her eyes fell to the scroll, lying near the burning carriage in the dirt at her feet. She should really get it away from the fire. . . .

All of a sudden she froze.

The prophecy.

The prophecy stated that the Chosen One would be saved. It said that she would be saved in a final hour of need. And there was a date under that passage. *Today's* date—

Her stomach plummeted.

As soon as she'd read those words Ibrahim had spotted the ship.

My God . . .

33

Downtown Seattle,
Washington
6:15 P.M.

"Caleb!" Ariel yelled in the fading twilight. "Caleb, *please!* Where are you?"

Nothing.

"Caleb! Caleb!"

But her hoarse cries went unanswered, ringing across the deserted streets and the glass walls of the empty skyscrapers. She must have shouted his name a thousand times. A *million* times. And all she heard were chirping crickets and squawking birds. It was like a goddamn zoo out here. She hadn't seen a single solitary human being all day long—which was kind of weird, actually. Usually she saw *somebody,* some random and emaciated teenager, wandering around like a zombie. Where the hell *was* everybody? Where was Caleb?

"Caleb!"

Maybe he's ignoring me on purpose.

Finally she slumped down on a curb. She couldn't go on. Her feet ached too much; her legs were too sore. She rested her elbows on her knees, allowing her head to droop.

"Come back, Caleb," she begged. Only now her cry

was little more than a whisper, aimed at the tarmac beneath her sneakers.

Why was he *doing* this?

A large and painful lump began to grow in her throat. Still, she couldn't bring herself to believe that he was really *gone*. No way. It was impossible. She *knew* him. Sure—maybe he was a little freaked by John's death. They *all* were. But he loved that lobby as much as any of them. He loved the nonstop partying, the private little universe they'd created.

Maybe he already went back.

Duh. Of course he went back. *Stupid.* Why hadn't she thought of that earlier? She'd been wandering these streets like a dope for hours instead of just using her head. A fleeting grin crossed her lips. He was probably already drunk again. Right?

She sniffed once and lifted her eyes.

"Caleb?" she yelled one last time, just for the hell of it.

Nah . . . he was home. After all, it was pretty dark. She should go home, too.

He *was* going to be there. Wasn't he?

She quickly scanned the avenue for a street sign, just to get her bearings—but all the lampposts and traffic lights were choked with vines. *Man.* She'd been too preoccupied to really notice . . . but the whole city was kind of creepy. Especially at night. Ever since the rain ended, Seattle had burst forth with wild plant life: bits of greenery that shot up through every available crack in the sidewalk and pavement. It wasn't a zoo out here. It was a *jungle*—

"Ariel?"

Caleb? She sprang to her feet.

"Over here," he called.

Her head jerked in the direction of the voice. *There!* She could see a skinny silhouette under a tree at the end of the street. Even in the shadow, there was no mistaking it.

"Caleb!" she shouted.

He waved. "Here I am."

The next instant she was sprinting toward him through the weeds, arms outstretched. *Okay, okay.* She couldn't get *that* worked up. She knew she'd find him sooner or later. But from now on, she would keep him on a tight leash. Yes. She would just have to hug him—squeeze him against her body so that he would never be able to wander off like that again.

"Hey," he called. He flashed a puzzled smile. "I heard you yelling. What are you doing all the way out here?"

Ariel jerked to a stop in front of him. "What do you mean?" she asked breathlessly. "I've been going *nuts!* I've been out here all day!"

He cocked an eyebrow. "You have?"

"Well . . ." Her arms sagged, falling to her sides. She awkwardly clasped her hands behind her back. "Not really . . . I mean, uh, I was—I was looking for you for a while."

"Oh." Suddenly his eyes brightened. "Ariel, you're not gonna believe it. I found the most incredible place."

The most incredible place? Ariel shook her head. "Caleb—"

"Come on, I'll show you right now," he interrupted.

"Wait, Caleb, are you okay?" she asked tentatively. "I mean . . . how do you feel?"

The old, familiar goofy grin appeared on his face. "I feel great. Come on."

He turned, but she reached out and grabbed his arm.

"Hold on." She peered at him closely. "I just . . . I don't know. What about John? I mean—not to be harsh or anything, but . . ."

"John?"

"Yeah." She locked gazes with him. "John."

He shrugged. "The guy melted, Ariel. What do you want me to say?"

What the— Ariel let go of his arm, flabbergasted. "Are you stoned or something?"

"No!" He started to laugh. "Look, let me just introduce you to these people. They're right around the corner. As soon as you meet them you'll understand."

Her eyes narrowed. "What do you mean, I'll *understand?*"

"Everybody's there, Ariel," he stated. "The entire city. Except us."

Ariel blinked a few times, swallowing. All right. She needed a quick time-out here. Was *she* going crazy? No . . . no, it was Caleb. Clearly something majorly wacked had happened to him. Like he'd been brainwashed. Or lobotomized. He sounded as if he'd joined one of those cults where they made you surrender all your money and worship some deranged billionaire who believes in UFOs. She kept staring at him. He *looked* the same. Well, it was dark out, but still . . .

"You didn't answer my question," she finally said.

He rolled his eyes. Then he grabbed her hand and

yanked it. The next thing she knew, she was stumbling along behind him.

"Hey!" she snapped. She fought to pull free, but he wouldn't let go. "Stop it. I'm serious, Caleb. It isn't funny—"

"Shhh," Caleb whispered. "You gotta chill, Ariel."

That was it. With a vicious twist she wrenched her hand out of his grasp, then stopped dead in her tracks. "In case you forgot, *you're* the one who flipped out and bolted from the lobby this morning," she barked. "*You* chill."

Caleb sighed, but he didn't stop to wait for her. He just kept walking toward the next intersection. "It would take me too long to explain everything, all right?" He turned and shuffled backward, waving his arm at something around the corner—something hidden behind an ivy-covered brick building. "Lemme just *show* you."

For a moment Ariel refused to budge.

"Come on!" he yelled.

Finally she clenched her jaw and stomped through the knee-high mesh of leaves. Obviously he wasn't going to take no for an answer. Obviously he was in a serious state of denial about John's death. She knew all about denial. She'd gotten an A in Intro to Psych.

Whatever this is, it better be good, she thought. She avoided his eyes as she rounded the corner. *It better be pretty damn good to make him act so—*

"See?" Caleb thrust his finger toward a towering, slender skyscraper at the end of the block.

Ariel gasped.

It looked exactly the same as any other building—except for one crucial difference.

There were *lights* in the windows.

Real lights. Not candles, not bonfires—but actual electric bulbs. There was a noise, too. It was very faint and muffled. She strained her ears. *Music!*

The thump of bass . . . it was house music, wasn't it? Something like that. She hadn't heard music since New Year's Eve. Not at all. Not a single note or drumbeat or chord. Amazing. She used to hate house music. Now it sounded like the sweetest thing in the world. . . .

Wait. Didn't she know this place?

Yeah, she did. She almost laughed out loud. It was the Sheraton Seattle Hotel and Towers, on 6th and Pike. Babylon High was supposed to have its senior prom here. It was kind of hard to recognize with all the ivy creeping up the side . . . but this was the spot, all right.

Caleb grabbed her arm again. "See what I mean?" he said, tugging her toward the doors. "I freaked out when I saw it, too. But wait till you get inside."

Whoa. She kept shaking her head as she trotted along beside him. A dozen questions festered in her mind. Who *lived* here? Who got the electricity running? Was it somebody like Trevor—or maybe even Trevor himself? Anything was possible. For a brief moment she even thought she could understand why Caleb was acting so strange. *She* felt strange just looking at this building.

"How?" she breathed. "How'd they . . ." She didn't even know what she wanted to ask.

"You gotta meet this girl Leslie," Caleb muttered quickly. "She was telling me all about it. You're gonna love her, Ariel. Seriously. She's just like—like you." He spoke so fast that he tripped over his words. "She just got here, too. She met all these guys who came up from Portland. They found this old generator and fixed it. It's crazy, Ariel. I mean . . . they got a Jacuzzi that *works*. They got washers and dryers. And just listen! That's the hotel *disco*. They crank tunes all the time. Leslie says we can each have a room to ourselves. . . ."

Sounds like heaven. For some reason, the more Caleb jabbered, the more she wanted to turn around. Everything about the hotel seemed . . . well, too good to be true. She couldn't say exactly what bothered her, either—except that it had a lot to do with the way Caleb was acting. Like the way he totally forgot about John. Nothing he'd said so far even came *close* to explaining why he was being so weird. What had this ultraperfect Leslie done to him, anyway?

"Here we go!" Caleb pushed through a pair of big glass double doors into a brightly lit lobby. It was pretty fancy—with chandeliers and plush carpeting and sofas and oak tables . . . except for the scraggly kids, of course. Dozens of boys were there, gathered around some girl.

"There's Leslie," Caleb whispered.

Ariel froze. *Yuck.* What was Caleb thinking?

Something was *definitely* wrong with him. This girl was *not* just like Ariel. Ariel didn't have curly jet black hair and dark bug eyes. Sure, Leslie was good-looking . . . but in a totally heinous and slutty kind of way. She was wearing these ridiculous black fish-net tights, a black miniskirt, and a black tank top. It didn't make sense. She just wasn't Caleb's *type*.

"Hey, Leslie!" Caleb called.

Leslie's eyes flashed to the two of them. Her dark, tanned face lit up.

"Caleb!" she cried, wriggling out of the circle of boys. She rushed over and draped her arms around him. "You came back! Right on, baby!"

Baby? Ariel frowned. *You gotta be kidding me.*

Caleb smiled. Then he planted a huge, wet, sloppy kiss right on her lips.

Ariel's jaw dropped. He'd just met this chick—and they were already swapping spit? *Forget it.* He *must* be stoned.

Leslie leaned back and smiled at Ariel. "And you must be his little friend," she said in a rich, singsong voice. "My name's Leslie. Leslie Arliss Irma Tisch."

That clinches it, Ariel thought. *It's time to get the hell out of here.* What a pretentious loser! If Ariel had four names (four ugly names, to boot), there was no way she'd spew them all out. What kind of a name was *Irma?* And Ariel was not Caleb's "little friend," whatever that meant. Right now she wasn't sure if she wanted to be friends with Caleb at *all*, actually.

"Um . . . this is Ariel," Caleb mumbled in the silence.

Leslie's smile widened. "Ariel what?"

"Ariel. Just Ariel. Period." She shot a hard glance at Caleb. "Don't you think we should be getting back home?"

Caleb giggled. He sounded like an idiot. "Home? I haven't been home in months."

"I mean the Citicorp building," she stated pointedly.

"Why don't you just hang here?" Leslie asked.

Ariel bit her lip. It took every ounce of self-control she had not to turn around and smack the girl. But she refused to cause a scene. No. She was going to remain calm and collected.

"Yeah, Ariel." Caleb's smile faded. "What's the big deal?"

"The big *deal?*" Ariel snapped.

Leslie laughed lightly. "Hey, whatever. It's cool. Do what you wanna do. I'm gonna show Caleb the disco."

Before Ariel could even utter a word, Leslie was whisking Caleb across the lobby, past the circle of kids, and through an ornate wooden door near a bank of elevators.

"Caleb, wait!" Ariel shouted. "Don't—"

The door slammed.

Ariel blinked. She couldn't believe it.

No way. No way are they gonna get away with making me look like a fool. . . .

Seething, she marched to the door and gave the shiny silver knob a ferocious twist.

Nothing happened. She frowned, jiggling it once, twice. But it still wouldn't budge.

She was locked out.

PART II:

April 2–17

Sheraton Seattle
Hotel and Towers
Morning of April 2

Caleb Walker wasn't used to feeling so mixed up.

Usually his *body* felt lousy and his *brain* felt decent. Usually his mood was up, up, up. Yes, sir. He was a regular Mr. Happy, a regular Barney the Dinosaur. How did the song go? *"I love you; you love me. . . ."* Right. That was how he usually felt. All the drinking and drugs kept the perma-grin stuck on his face. In the meantime his brain cells died, his liver decomposed, and his hands shook so much that he could barely even light a cigarette.

Not today, though. Today his body felt like a million bucks. Especially in the Jacuzzi.

So why couldn't he muster a smile? One stupid smile?

Sure, he was a little sore. Last night he'd danced like a wild man—shaking his booty for about eight hours straight. He'd been stone-cold sober, too. He hadn't exercised that much in months. He felt like the host of *The Grind* or something. But now the Jacuzzi was soothing him, taking care of the aches and pains and strained muscles, while the steamy water and hot bubble jets made his skin feel like a layer of melted butter. . . .

Aaahhh.

47

That's what he *should* have been saying.

Enjoy yourself, dammit! He propped his elbows up on the white tile edge of the tub, then closed his eyes and furiously tried to luxuriate in the morning sunlight streaming through the skylight. But no—that didn't work, either. He still felt all agitated and unsettled. There was a weird, unpleasant emptiness in his stomach. Usually at this late hour of the morning he was ravenously hungry. He could eat an entire box of cereal in about two minutes flat. Today he had no appetite at all.

It's all Ariel's fault, he thought angrily. *Why did she wig out? Why did she have to bring up John? I almost managed to forget about all that. If she just let me explain—*

"Caleb?"

His eyes popped open.

Then his heart nearly stopped.

God help me. Leslie was standing before him, wearing possibly the skimpiest black bikini he had ever seen. She might as well have been naked. He fought to stare at her face—*only* her face—but it was extremely difficult. Her body was perfect. *Perfect.* She looked like a photograph of some supermodel come to life.

"I thought you'd be here," she said with a sly smile.

She carefully slipped into the water beside him. It was only then that he noticed she was holding something—a huge cocktail glass filled with a pulpy red tomato drink, complete with a straw and one of those little paper umbrellas.

A Bloody Mary. Caleb's mouth watered. Hot diggity. *That* would take his mind off his troubles. It had been a while since he'd had one of those.

"Sleep all right?" she asked.

Caleb nodded. The truth was that he hadn't slept at all. He'd gone straight from the disco to this hot tub. But why get into it? He was wide awake.

"Good." She thrust the glass toward him. "Here. I brought you a little something for breakfast."

"Uh . . . thanks," he mumbled. Suddenly he was extremely conscious of the fact that he was wearing only a pair of ratty boxer shorts. The rest of his clothes lay in a heap by the door. Well, the vodka in the Bloody Mary would help him forget about that, too. He gingerly plucked the glass from her hand, then shoved the straw into his mouth and slurped as fast as he could—

"Blecchh!" he cried.

He spat the straw out of his mouth, coughing.

His face shriveled. This was *not* a cocktail. It tasted like *clams* or something. And there was no booze in it at all. . . .

"What's wrong? You don't like Clamato juice?"

He blinked a few times, brushing wet strands of hair out of his rapidly reddening face. No, he didn't like Clamato juice. But that wasn't the point. The point was that the horrible taste caught him completely by surprise—and now he looked like a major fool.

"Are you okay?" she pressed.

"Yeah, yeah," he stammered, placing the glass on the tile behind him. He smiled weakly. "It's just, I thought it—I thought it was, um . . . a . . ."

Leslie raised her eyebrows. "Was a what?"

"You know," he mumbled. "Like a Bloody Mary or something."

"A Bloody Mary?" She laughed. Her voice was teasing. "Damn, Caleb. You really like to start the day with a bang, huh?"

He shrugged and lowered his eyes. *Way to go, man. Real suave.* Maybe he should just shut his mouth. He gazed down at his puny chest. *That* pitiful sight didn't do much to improve his mood, either. The state of his body was not good. He had no muscle definition, just a layer of pallid and booze-saturated flab over bones. It was pathetic. He looked like a wasteoid in one of those antidrug public-service announcements they used to have: *"Do drugs and you'll end up like this!"* No wonder he felt like crap all the time.

What had happened to him? He used to play varsity basketball. He used to be an *athlete*.

"I'm just busting on you, Caleb," Leslie apologized. "Sorry. I don't mean to be harsh."

"No, no." He glanced up and shook his head. "You're right. I mean . . . I'm so used to starting the day with a drink that it seems totally natural." A shameful little grin passed over his lips. "And *that* is pretty damn depressing."

Leslie shrugged casually. "Not really. I have tons of friends who party really hard. It's just that . . . I don't know. We got what—two years left, three years left? You know, if the plague keeps up or whatever. And I don't want to waste any of that time. I want to be *sharp*. You know what I'm saying?"

With that she quickly ducked her head under the

frothy surface. Then she popped back up—eyes closed, back arched, brushing her long, wet black hair behind her shoulders. Steaming water dripped from her flawless body. . . .

Caleb swallowed. *Wow.*

Just looking at her made him really, really nervous. He totally forgot what they were just talking about. He felt a little dizzy, in fact. Maybe he'd been in the tub for too long. Maybe he should get out before he made an even *bigger* fool of himself.

With a soft splash Leslie settled back into her seat. She shot a quick smile at him. "What are you thinking?" she asked.

His eyes fell away from her, back to the bubbles. What could he say? That he'd sell his soul to the devil for just one chance to jump her bones?

"Hey, Caleb?" she said quietly. "Is everything okay? You seem kind of bummed."

Caleb hesitated. *As a matter of fact, I am,* he thought. But he didn't exactly want to bore her with the lame details of his life.

"I'm sorry," she murmured. "It's none of my business—"

Caleb shook his head. "It's okay. . . ."

"It's your friend, right? The chick who took off? Ariel?"

"It's just that she didn't give me a chance to explain," he blurted. The words seemed to burst out of his mouth before he could even help himself. "I mean, I know that she must have been worried and stuff. I *did* just run out of the lobby yesterday without saying anything." He sighed, then glanced back up at Leslie. "I guess I could have handled it better. I just didn't want to deal."

She nodded. "You didn't want to deal with that weird funeral-type thing for your friend John. The ceremony you were telling me about. Is that it?"

"Exactly." He raised his hands, splashing the hot water. It was amazing: Leslie seemed to understand everything. "I mean, part of the reason I want to stay *here* is because you said that nobody here makes a big deal when people melt. They just toss the clothes in the garbage and get on with their lives. And I can totally relate to that. I don't want people to stop having fun when *I* die. I want them to concentrate on the *good* stuff—on living, you know? There isn't enough time for anything else." Leslie sighed. "I know. If I stood in a circle and took one thing from every single friend who *I* saw die . . ." She laughed shortly. "Well, I wouldn't have anywhere to put it all. But I think I'd also end up getting seriously depressed. I mean, like so depressed that I'd want to kill myself or something."

"That's how I feel!" Caleb exclaimed. "That's why I had to get out of there. If Ariel just gave me the chance to tell her . . ."

A silence fell between them.

"Is Ariel your girlfriend?" Leslie asked in a casual tone.

Caleb shook his head. "No," he stated emphatically. "No way. I mean, we're just friends. . . ." His voice trailed off. There was a time—not too long ago, in fact—when he thought that Ariel would make an awesome girlfriend. Or at least a cool girl to fool around with. He'd thought about it a lot, actually. But the opportunity never presented itself. The lobby wasn't exactly the most private place in the world. And after last night . . .

"Can I ask you something, Caleb?"

"Sure," he said.

She smiled hesitantly. "I don't know. You might get offended."

"I doubt it."

Leslie took a deep breath. "Ariel isn't one of those people, who, like, believe in the Chosen One or anything, is she?"

Caleb laughed. "Why would that offend me?"

"I don't know." Leslie absently ran her fingers across the surface of the water. "A lot of people take that kind of thing really seriously. I mean, nobody *I* hang out with . . ."

"Nobody I hang out with, either," Caleb mumbled. "Especially Ariel. Actually, when I first met her, she was living with a bunch of weirdos who *did* believe in the Chosen One." He chuckled, mostly to himself. "She wasn't too happy about it, either. She used to rag on them in this really funny way. . . ." Once again he left the sentence hanging. His smile faded. Why did that seem like so long ago?

"Hey, you know what?" Leslie suddenly asked. She jumped up and sloshed out of the tub, then hurried toward the exit, her wet footsteps smacking on the tile. "Let's forget about it. I got something that'll cheer you up. One second."

Caleb stared at her butt as she disappeared out the door.

Just being allowed to hang out with you is enough to cheer me up.

Too bad he didn't he have the guts to say something like that. Well, not something *exactly* like that—because that was way too cheesy. But something nice and sweet . . .

A moment later she reappeared, holding a thick, battered book in her dripping hand. She quickly hopped back into the water.

"Check this out," she said excitedly. She sidled up beside him, carefully holding the book above the surface—but the pages were all wrinkled, as if they'd already gotten wet a few times. "I found this out in the woods, up by the Snohomish River."

A smile crossed Caleb's face. His eyes widened. At first he thought his mind was playing tricks on him.

The title of the book read: *Skintight: The Illustrated History of Erotic Film.*

"Whoa," he mumbled.

Leslie giggled. "That's what I said."

She began slowly flipping the pages. Caleb smirked. The book was really poorly manufactured. Most of the pictures were blurry and cheaply reproduced. Still, some of them were pretty explicit. A lot of them were funny. A lot of them were downright *gross.* Caleb's eyes narrowed. Some of the scenes involved three or more people. . . .

"I didn't even know that this stuff was legal," Caleb muttered. He glanced at Leslie.

She was actually *blushing.* Her dark cheeks were flushed with a soft glow.

54

"What?" Caleb teased. "Does this kind of thing embarrass you?"

She shook her head. "No," she murmured. "It turns me on."

Oh, Lord . . .

Caleb swallowed. His heart felt as if it were about to fly right out of his chest. Why did she have to say something like that? Couldn't she see that she was driving him insane? He stared at her, desperately struggling to think of something witty to say, something sexy, something to make her *act* on that statement . . . but he felt like a dog with his tongue hanging out of his mouth.

"It does?" he finally managed. His voice was thick.

She closed the book and tossed it out of the tub. It landed with a loud *thwack*.

"Mm-hmm. Don't you want to try it out?"

His breath started coming fast. "What do you mean?" he croaked.

"Oh, I don't know," she whispered huskily. She turned and wrapped her arms around his neck, pressing her body against his. "Use your imagination. . . ."

Caleb closed his eyes. He felt her lips press against his own—but incredibly he was only dimly aware of kissing her. Reality seemed very far away.

All he could think was: *How did I pull this off?*

CHAPTER SIX

Carnival cruise ship *The Majestic*,
Southeast Mediterranean
Evening of April 2

"Sprechen Sie Deutsch?" the uniformed teenage soldier barked at Sarah.

Sarah gaped at him uncomprehendingly.

"Parlez-vous français?"

"Uh . . ." Sarah shook her head.

The boy's face darkened. His grip tightened on the machine gun slung over his shoulder. Then his eyes flashed to Ibrahim. *"Techkee Ingleesi?"*

"Yes, yes," Ibrahim answered. "English."

"D'accord," the boy mumbled, nodding. He yanked a roll of white tape from a utility pack around his waist, then tore off a strip and slapped it onto Ibrahim's bare wrist. After another harsh glance at the both of them he disappeared up the metal stairs, his combat boots clanging noisily.

"What was that all about?" Sarah whispered.

Ibrahim shrugged. "I guess they want to know what language we speak. Maybe they'll send somebody who speaks English to tell us what's going on."

They'd better, she thought desperately. She turned and surveyed the crowded, windowless cabin. Claustrophobia was beginning to take its toll. If she had to stay down belowdecks much longer, crammed in with the rest of these restless, hungry, frightened kids . . . she didn't know *what* she'd do. She hadn't seen the sun since she'd been hauled aboard. And it was so noisy in here—teeming with the barks and grunts of a dozen languages she couldn't understand. Who was in charge? What *was* this ship? They'd been down here for a full twenty-four hours, an entire *day,* and still nobody had explained what was going on.

"Are you okay?" Ibrahim asked.

Sarah chewed a fingernail. "I don't know."

He bent over and picked up a nearly empty plastic bottle of water. "Here," he said, swishing the dregs in her face. "Drink this."

She shook her head. "I'm not thirsty."

"You sure?" His sweaty brow grew furrowed. Dark circles ringed his eyes. "It's important to stay hydrated."

"Then how come they only gave us *one* bottle of water?" she yelled.

Ibrahim reached out and placed a moist hand on her shoulder. "Sarah, please," he soothed. "The situation will improve. I promise."

How do you know? she thought, but she kept silent. She knew she shouldn't take it out on Ibrahim. The truth was that she *was* thirsty. She just didn't want to have to go to the bathroom again. The ladies' room down here had only one working toilet—and the stench of the place was enough to make her vomit. Not that she'd have anything *to* vomit; the soldiers had given her only one sticky, half-melted candy bar since she'd come on board. And the men's room was locked. It was absurd. One working toilet for hundreds of kids! On a cruise ship! But she could just bet that those soldiers had *plenty* of toilets and *plenty* of water upstairs. . . .

"You know what?" she muttered, half to herself. "I'm beginning to wish we *hadn't* been rescued. We'd probably be dead by now, and the whole thing would be over—"

"Don't say that!" Ibrahim cried. "You saw the prophecy!"

Sarah opened her mouth . . . but no words would come. An unpleasant tingle crept up her spine. Yes, she'd seen the prophecy. She'd also had plenty of time to think about it, too.

Am I . . . ?

When they signaled the ship yesterday, there was little doubt in her mind that the prophecies referred to *her*. The coincidences were simply too powerful to deny. She *had* to be the Chosen One. Why else would she have ended up with the scroll? Everything fit: the way she'd been saved, the way she'd miraculously survived the attack on Elijah's house, the way fate had brought her to Ibrahim's estate and converted her into a true believer in the prophecies. . . .

The scroll was a road map of her life. The rescue had been a final sign, a revelation.

But now she wasn't so sure. Had she really been rescued? *Captured* was more like it. And she didn't

59

feel any different or special, like some kind of savior. No, she felt like another faceless waif in a bewildered and angry mob.

"You're the Chosen One, Sarah," Ibrahim stated in a low voice. "I know you are. I saw your face in a vision, remember? *Your* face."

She met his gaze for a moment, then averted her eyes. How could somebody else be so sure who she was? *She* wasn't even sure. . . .

Uh-oh.

Someone was staring at them.

It was a girl: a fair-skinned redhead, standing barefoot near the staircase in a grubby sundress. She was looking at the piece of tape on Ibrahim's hand.

"What?" Sarah demanded.

The girl looked up at her. "I—I'm sorry," she stammered awkwardly. "It's just that I heard you talking, and I wanted to make sure . . ." She didn't finish.

"Make sure of *what?*" Sarah snapped.

"That you spoke English." She tried to smile, but she looked troubled, uncomfortable. Her light blue eyes kept darting around the room. "They stick white tape on everybody who speaks English." She raised the back of her hand to reveal her own small strip. "See? It's so they can tell us apart from the rest—"

"Who are *they?*" Sarah interrupted.

The girl blinked. "Uh . . . you know," she answered meekly.

"No, I *don't* know," Sarah growled. "Sorry to be

rude—but we've been down here for a whole day now, and nobody's told us a thing."

The girl glanced between Sarah and Ibrahim. Her eyes narrowed. "They haven't told you *anything?*"

"No!" Sarah shouted.

"Oh, dear," the girl mumbled. Her forehead was tightly creased. "So you don't know about the lottery?"

Sarah shook her head. "The lottery?"

"I mean, it's okay . . . because, uh, it has nothing to do with us," the girl said quickly. "We speak English. We automatically get to stay on board. They need English speakers when they get to the States."

"The *States?*" Sarah cried, forgetting her anger. An electric excitement coursed through her veins. She couldn't believe it. This ship was going *home!* It was a miracle. She never thought she'd get back to America. *Ever.* Her parents, her friends . . .

The girl didn't say anything else. All of a sudden she looked very afraid.

"Okay—just please start from the top," Sarah said. She took a deep breath, fighting to remain calm. "Tell us who you are, and who they are, and what the story is with this ship. Then *we'll* answer any questions *you* have. All right?"

"I'm sorry." The girl nodded tentatively, then stole a quick peek over her shoulder—up the stairs. "Well, uh . . . my name's Aviva, but that doesn't really matter." She turned back to them and spoke in rapid, hushed tones. "I was in Gaza when the flood hit. Next thing I know, I'm holding on to a piece of wood in the middle of the ocean. The soldiers rescued me. They're part of a UN battalion stationed in Greece. They took over this ship and—"

"A UN battalion?" Ibrahim interrupted. "Does the UN still exist?"

Aviva shook her head. "No. These guys are the only ones left. They're all our age, just like everywhere else around here." She lowered her voice to a whisper. "They were headed to the United States. But then the Red Sea flooded. So they changed course and came to look for survivors." She closed her eyes for a moment. *"Baruch Hashem."*

"Wait!" Sarah's eyes widened. *Hebrew!* She stepped toward Aviva. "Are you Israeli?"

Aviva nodded.

"Do you know what's happening in Jerusalem?" Sarah asked, seized with a sudden urgency. If this girl came from Israel, then there was a chance—however minuscule—that she might have come across Josh. "Were you there?"

"No. I was in Bethlehem. I headed south as soon as the disease hit. The whole country is a war zone. I doubt there's much of anything left."

Sarah blinked. A strange coldness settled over her body. *A war zone.* She shuddered. So there was no hope for Josh. None.

"What is this lottery you spoke of?" Ibrahim demanded.

Aviva's face grew even paler. "That's the thing. When they came to rescue people, the ship was already overloaded. They can't bring everyone to

America—they don't have enough supplies for the trip. So they're going to hold a lottery. Whoever picks the right number gets to stay on board. Whoever doesn't gets left behind when we reach Crete."

Ibrahim nodded. "That seems fair."

Aviva bit her lip. "Except—" She paused for a moment. "You know about America, don't you?"

America? Sarah frowned at Ibrahim. He shrugged.

"Nobody caught the disease there," Aviva whispered. "Everything is exactly the same. There are adults, and a government, and civilization. The kids who get left behind might not survive on Crete. But everyone who stays on board gets to live in the real world, the *old* world, where it's safe."

Sarah gasped. "How do you know?"

"Everybody knows," Aviva mumbled. "The ship has been picking up TV broadcasts and radio reports—"

"Faites-attention!" a voice barked from the top of the stairs.

Aviva jerked violently. A look of terror crossed her face.

"What's going on?" Sarah asked.

But Aviva didn't answer. She scrambled away from the stairwell, cowering behind Ibrahim as five angry-looking boys in full camouflage combat regalia marched down the stairs, machine guns drawn. Three of them also held small buckets in their hands. The buckets were filled with small folded slips of white paper.

63

"Faites-attention!" one of the boys yelled again.

The packed room fell silent. All eyes turned to the stairwell.

"La loterie commence maintenant," another soldier announced. Sarah stole a quick glance at Aviva. *Jeez.* The girl was shaking, white as a sheet. What had they done to scare her so much?

The soldiers began to move among the crowd, shoving the buckets in the kids' faces. Slowly, shakily, the kids dipped their hands into the papers. Their faces were masks of fear. There was a split second where everyone seemed to be holding their breath. . . .

How can people do this to each other? Sarah wondered. *How can they be so cruel? It's almost like deciding who gets to live and who gets to die. How would it feel to be left behind, knowing this ship is heading back to civilization without you?*

And then, an instant later, the room erupted. Wails of sorrow and shouts of joy filled the hot, stale air. Sarah's unbelieving eyes flashed from one soldier to the next—one standing before a couple in which the girl had clearly won but the boy hadn't . . . one standing before a group of girls who were all pleading for a second chance . . . one standing before a boy who suddenly fainted. . . .

It's inhuman. It isn't right. I just thank God I'm not a part of it—

And then one of the soldiers stepped in front of Sarah. He was a beefy kid who must have weighed two hundred pounds. He didn't have a bucket. He glanced down at her hand, then Ibrahim's, then Aviva's.

"You two," he said, waving the tip of his rifle at Aviva and Ibrahim. He spoke with a thick French accent. "Go upstair wiz me."

Sarah frowned. "What about me?"

"No." The boy stood rigid, blocking her path. His eyes were totally void of emotion. "Only white upstair."

"But *listen* to me," she protested. She almost laughed. "I speak English."

"Only white upstair," he repeated. He gazed at her, unblinking.

Ibrahim tried to maneuver between them. "There must be some kind of mistake," he said, forcing a smile. "Nobody ever spoke to Sarah in English, so they didn't know to give her—"

"What's the problem?" another soldier interrupted.

Sarah breathed a sigh of relief. This one's accent was British, not French. *Here* was somebody who could sort this out. "It's just a mistake," she explained as he strode toward her. "You forgot to give me a strip of white tape."

He sneered. "A *mistake?*"

Sarah nodded. "Yeah. It's okay."

"No white tape," he stated tersely. He glanced at her hand. "You stay for the lottery."

For a moment the words didn't seem to register. What was his problem? She *spoke* his language. What was so important about a piece of stupid tape?

"You don't get it," she argued, her voice rising. "I'm an Ameri—"

"Shut up," he snarled. He jerked his head toward the French officer. *"Allez-y."*

The French soldier nodded. He slung his rifle over his shoulder. Then he seized Ibrahim and Aviva by the upper arms and roughly dragged them toward the stairs.

"Get off of me!" Ibrahim shouted, squirming. "She has to come with us!"

Without a word of warning the British soldier took three quick steps toward Ibrahim and slammed the butt of his rifle against the back of Ibrahim's neck.

Ibrahim instantly collapsed to the floor. Blood trickled from a gash below his hairline.

Oh, my God.

A horrified whimper escaped Sarah's lips. Her knees began to tremble. *This can't be happening. . . .*

Aviva bolted up the stairs.

The room was perfectly still.

"Let me tell you something," the British soldier stated in calm tones, turning back to Sarah. "Our duty is to *obey* the orders of our commanding officer. Not to interpret those orders. Do you understand?"

The color drained from Sarah's face. She couldn't answer. She couldn't tear her eyes from Ibrahim. She simply stared in mute terror as the French soldier lifted him off the ground and slung him over his shoulder like a sack of potatoes—then disappeared up the stairs. These soldiers were insane. She felt a sudden dreaded certainty that she would lose the lottery, that she'd be dropped at Crete, that she'd never see her parents or her home again. . . .

"But I will make an exception in your case," he added.

Sarah turned to him.

He smiled coldly. "I'm taking you out of the lottery altogether. You won't be making the journey with us to the States. In case you forgot, *we* saved *your* life. We owe you nothing. So you can serve as an example to the others of what happens when passengers complain about the rules."

SEVEN

**Route 317,
near Amarillo, Texas
Afternoon of April 10**

I have a secret. I don't want to tell George, either, because I don't want to make him any more worried than he already is. But I'm scared.

I know that's nothing new. I've been scared in one way or another since New Year's Eve. Even before, really. And I'm sure that everybody else in the world is scared right now, too. But this is different. It has nothing to do with the plague.

Or, on the other hand, it has everything to do with the plague.

I'm scared because I can't

69

remember who the old Julia Morrison was. That's my secret.

Sometimes I look in the rearview mirror at myself and find that I'm looking at somebody I've never met. I ask myself: Who is this person? Who is this girl who sees things and hears voices and feels like there's a huge magnet pulling her toward an unknown place? It's not _me_. It can't be ME. So where is Julia?

Only two weeks ago I was the happiest person in the world. Wasn't I? No more visions, no more dreams, no more nothing. Just George . . .

Then there was the flood, and the rain ended, and I was crazy again.

How many days have I been on the road now? How many months?

I don't even know. All I know is that we aren't getting anywhere. We've been driving in circles for days. Every time we try to go west, the road is blocked. There are fires everywhere. Brushfires, forest fires, burning piles of trash in the middle of the highways. I don't understand it. How did they start? It's like somebody set them on purpose, just to drive us crazy.

And for all I know, that may be true.

But I have George. I have to keep reminding myself of how lucky I am for that. I think a lot about Luke and all the things he did to me. He put me through hell. We never <u>shared</u> anything. George and I have been through hell <u>together</u>. We share everything. Even our visions. He's *saved my life more than once. I know I'm older, and we come from two totally different worlds, but it doesn't matter. I love him*

"Hey, Julia, check this out," George called from the front seat.

Julia glanced up from her diary. "What is it?"

"I don't know. There's this weird sign up ahead. . . ."

George shifted gears. The car slowed for a moment. Julia closed the worn little book, then sat up straight and leaned between the two front seats.

"See what I mean?" George asked. He pointed to a billboard on the right side of the road.

She squinted at the sign in the afternoon glare. He was right; it *was* weird. For one thing, it was the only man-made object out here, as far as she could see. It seemed really odd and out of place—standing alone on the two-lane highway, towering over the endless sea of cornfields. And whatever had originally been advertised was now hidden under a coat of sloppy white paint. Over that somebody had sprayed the words: The Time to Repent Is Now!

George snickered. "I guess we really hit the Bible Belt, huh?"

"I guess so," she mumbled. She watched as the billboard whizzed past the window, catching a glimpse of a distant fire on the horizon and a plume of smoke rising up toward the setting sun. *It never ends,* she thought. She shook her head. "Where are we, anyway?"

"Texas. We crossed the border about an hour ago. I saw a sign a few miles back for Amarillo. Wanna stop there for the night?"

"Sure," she murmured. She yawned and leaned back into the seat. She *was* pretty tired, she supposed. She wasn't even sure why; she'd been dozing in the backseat for most of the day. But it would be dark in a few hours. She wondered for a moment if they'd meet anybody in Amarillo—any crazies, any hoodlums, any lost and desperate kids like themselves . . . or if they'd just find a cozy little bed in an empty house where they could curl up, just the two of them, and forget about life. Wouldn't that be perfect?

"Hey, here's another one," George called over his shoulder. He chuckled. "Whoever lived around here musta seen too many religious TV shows."

Julia peered out the window again. Another whitewashed billboard was rapidly approaching. This, too, had a spray-painted message. It read: Entering the Promised Land! Submit to the Healer and He Will Grant You Eternal Life!

"The promised land?" Julia asked, frowning.

George didn't say anything. Instead he slowed the car.

Julia turned from the billboard. *Uh-oh.*

Something was happening up ahead.

A group of a dozen or so kids stood in the middle of the road, frantically waving and jumping up and down. Was there some kind of accident? Julia's eyes narrowed. They were all wearing the same thing. . . .

It looked like a white graduation gown.

"Whaddaya think?" George asked tonelessly. "Think I should stop?"

"I don't think you have a choice," she muttered.

As if on cue, the kids began running toward the car, their arms pumping in the air—a human tidal wave.

Julia swallowed. She could see now that they were smiling. So there was no reason to be scared, right? If they were smiling, they were friendly. Then again, most of the friendly-looking kids Julia had met in the past few months had turned out to be murderous psychopaths. But there was no way George could get around them unless he wanted to mow through all that corn. The Bug's little wheels would get stuck—

George hit the brakes. The car bounced to a stop.

In an instant the boys and girls were swarming upon them, surrounding them—clapping, laughing, dancing. A few of them pressed their faces against the windows. Julia flinched. They were *filthy*. Their gowns were caked with dirt. And Julia couldn't help but notice something else, too. Even though they were all dressed exactly the same, they were the most ethnically diverse bunch of kids she'd seen since she'd left New York: a mix of Caucasians, African Americans, Asians, Hispanics . . . like a mini-hodgepodge of the whole country.

Who are these people?

"Welcome!" they were shouting. "Welcome to the Promised Land!"

"You've been saved!"

"The Healer will bless you!"

"Damn," George whispered uneasily. He left the engine running. "What do we do now?"

Julia shook her head. "I—I . . . don't know," she stammered.

A short, sunburned girl knocked on Julia's door. Her smile was so wide that it looked unnatural—almost demented. Julia forced herself to roll down the window.

"Hi!" the girl cried.

"Um . . . hi," Julia mumbled.

"The Healer is waiting for you," the girl proclaimed. She sounded pleased with herself.

Waiting for me? Julia exchanged a quick glance with George. His green eyes darkened.

"How does the Healer know we're coming?" he demanded.

The girl laughed. "The Healer knows *everything*," she replied, as if that were the most ridiculous question she'd ever heard.

"Who is . . . the Healer?" Julia asked.

"Who is he?" The girl sighed. "A divine man. A man gifted with magic, a man of signs and wonders." Her voice grew dreamy. "I couldn't possibly explain. When you see him, you'll know."

Julia glanced at George again, then back at the girl. "Who are *you?*"

"The welcoming committee!" she cried. "Listen, everything will be explained once you get inside. Okay? Just follow the highway for another half mile and take a right at the dirt road. That's the Healer's home—"

"What if we don't want to go inside?" George

75

snapped.

The girl didn't even blink. If she was offended by George's curt tone, she didn't show it. She seemed completely unfazed. "The choice is yours," she said. "But I know you'd be making a mistake. I *know* that the Healer is the Chosen One, and—"

"*Wait!*" Julia and George both shouted at the same time.

Julia shot a wide-eyed look at George. She drew in her breath. "What do you mean, the Chosen One?" she demanded.

"That's what some of us in the Promised Land call him," the girl said.

"People you know?" George pressed.

She nodded enthusiastically. "They've *seen* him, you see. In visions—"

George slammed his fist on the horn. The tinny, high-pitched honk instantly silenced her. He yanked the gearshift and the car lurched forward with a screech. The rest of the kids scrambled out of the way.

"Are you gonna check it out?" Julia asked shakily.

He nodded, his eyes fixed on the road. "You bet."

"I thought the Chosen One was a girl," Julia breathed.

George lifted his shoulders. "Me too. But if people really have visions here . . ."

Seconds later a wide dirt road appeared in the midst of the corn on the right side of the highway. George spun the wheel. The Bug swerved off the pavement with a jolt. Julia gripped the side of the door. After they had bounced along for a few moments a tall red silo swam into view, followed by a dilapidated barn and a smallish wood frame house. The fields on either side of the road were packed with scores of kids in white gowns—planting, picking corn, tilling the soil.

All of them stopped and waved as George and Julia sped past. "This isn't the place I see in *my* visions," George muttered.

Julia rubbed her palms on her jeans. She didn't see anything like this, either. She saw a desert. Could this place really be important? She searched her feelings, but she couldn't tell; she was too unsettled. . . .

George pulled up in front of the silo. The area was deserted.

"I guess we should look for the Healer, huh?" he said. He cut the engine.

Julia nodded. She didn't know what to say.

They stepped out of the car, eyeing the place cautiously. Voices from the nearby fields drifted past on the breeze.

"Where do you think we should start?" Julia murmured.

"Beats the hell out of me," George mumbled. He looked up at the silo. Then he frowned. He began walking around it, craning his neck as he stared up at the tower.

"What's up?" Julia asked.

"There's something painted on the wall."

Julia followed him, shielding her eyes from the sun with her hand. *Wow.* George was right. Huge, dripping letters covered an entire side of the silo, from top to bottom. . . .

The Seven Commandments

1. The word of <u>the Healer</u> is absolute.

2. No one may speak against <u>the Healer.</u>

3. No one but <u>the Healer</u> shall attempt to heal anyone else.

4. No drugs or alcohol are permitted in the Promised Land except under supervision of <u>the Healer.</u> Abstinence is holy.

5. No sexual relations are permitted in the Promised Land unless sanctioned by <u>the Healer.</u> Purity is sacred.

6. No guns are permitted in the Promised Land.

7. Everyone must work the fields and scour the neighboring countryside for supplies. At the end of each week the flock must present the fruits of its labor to <u>the Healer.</u> No one is allowed to face <u>the Healer</u> empty-handed.

"What the hell kind of place *is* this?" George whispered.

Julia shook her head, aghast. "I don't know. . . ."

"These jerks are full of it," he grumbled. "No *way* is this guy the Chosen One."

For a moment Julia held her breath, frightened of what she was about to ask. Finally she exhaled. "Do you think this is a trap, George? Like that place in Jackson?"

"Maybe," he said, glowering at the painted words. "But I don't want to stick around to—"

"This is no trap," a deep voice interrupted from behind them.

Julia whirled around.

A guy in a white lab coat stood before them in the dirt. Julia gasped, instantly struck by how *old* he looked—unlike anyone else she'd seen in a long, long time—with high cheekbones and thoughtful blue eyes. Long brown hair tumbled over his shoulders. And he seemed healthy, too. His face had color; his body wasn't painfully thin, like hers. She couldn't stop staring at him. *Was* he older? She'd assumed everyone in their twenties was dead. But he didn't look like a teenager. He looked like a *man*. Hope flashed through her. If this guy had been spared the plague, maybe the Chosen One really *was* here. . . .

"Who are you?" George breathed.

"The Healer, of course," he replied with a smile. "Or the Chosen One, if you prefer. Even Doctor is okay. My given name is Dr. Harold Wurf. Welcome to the Promised Land."

CHAPTER EIGHT

**Sheraton Seattle
Hotel and Towers
Night of April 17**

In all her life, Ariel never once knew what it was to be an *outcast*. She never knew what it was like to feel shafted. Rejected. Spurned. Like she didn't measure up . . .

But standing here alone on this weed-choked boulevard in the middle of the night, with the hotel looming over her like a giant, glowing, pulsating jukebox—well, the message hit home pretty damn hard. Yup. There wasn't a lot of gray area.

I'm all alone in the world.

It was truly poetic, in a way. What was the word Mr. Wilson always used to toss around in English class . . . *metaphor*. Yeah. That was it. That was what the hotel was: a humongous, in-your-face *metaphor*. It perfectly symbolized how *she* was left out. Every single kid in Seattle was in there partying—except her. *Everybody*. Even Jared, Cynthia, and Marianne were there. They had long since abandoned the Citicorp lobby for the promise of electricity and clean sheets. And who could blame them?

I'm all alone in the world.

She chewed her lip, gazing up at the happy figures

in the windows. *Man.* She shouldn't have come here. She'd fought the temptation with everything she had. But in the end she had no choice. If she had stayed one more night in that lobby by herself, she would have died. *Literally.* She'd learned something in these past two weeks: People needed other people. Just like they needed food or oxygen. It wasn't a theory, either. It was a *fact.* Human contact was necessary for survival. Without it a person would wither and decay.

I'm all alone in the world.

It was funny: She'd even found herself longing for dear old Jezebel Howe. Her best friend. The very *first* person to ever ditch her for electricity and clean sheets, in fact. But why stay mad? After all, Ariel had always known that Jez looked out for only one person: Jez. That was why Ariel used to get such a kick out of her. Jez was selfishness incarnate. Miz Me-myself-and-I. Hell, Ariel had almost even *forgiven* her.

Almost.

Isolation really worked wonders, didn't it?

More than a few times in the past two weeks Ariel found herself wondering what would happen if she went back home to Babylon and tried to make amends with Trevor. Would he let her into his sick little compound at the Washington Institute of Technology? Was it even *there* anymore? Maybe he would just shoot her—

"Hey, Ariel!" a voice shouted, snapping her out of her reverie. "Hey!"

Jared.

He was standing in front of the double doors at the hotel entrance, waving at her excitedly. A grin

82

crossed her face. It felt pretty damn nice to see him, to see *anyone*. It felt even better to hear somebody say her name.

"Come *here!*" he cried, waving her over.

She trotted up the steps and into the light.

Well, well, well. It was also kind of nice to see that two weeks of clean sheets and hot showers hadn't done Jared much good. He still had the same scruff, the same sacks under his eyes, the same long greasy hair. Maybe the hotel wasn't all it was cracked up to be.

"How's it going, Jared?" she asked.

"Great!" He breathed a long, exaggerated sigh of relief. "God, Ariel . . . I'm so psyched you came. I was beginning to get worried about you. Really."

Ariel flashed a brittle smile. *Nice try. If you were worried, all you had to do was go back to the Citicorp lobby.*

"So how's it going?" he pushed. "What've you been up to?"

"Oh—same old, same old," she replied breezily. "So. Have you seen Caleb?"

Jared nodded. "Yeah, he's upstairs with Leslie in their room." He laughed, then shook his head. "God, you look great—"

"Hold up," she interrupted. "Did you say *their* room?"

"Yeah, they've been crashing up on the twentieth floor in one of those executive suites." He raised his eyebrows. "It's pretty phat, actually. They got a king-size bed and a whirlpool in the bathtub. . . ."

Their room. Ariel stared at him, hardly listening

83

as he continued to babble about the fabulous amenities—in *their room*. The room they shared. The two of them.

". . . a CD player and a VCR, too—"

"You say they're up there right now?" Ariel cut in. Jared nodded.

Before he could further elaborate, she shoved her way through the double doors and strode across the soft carpeting to the elevators. A small crowd of kids were gathered there, hanging out and drinking. She didn't so much as glance at them. She didn't even so much as look back in Jared's direction. *Of all the sick things . . .*

"Ariel, wait up!" Jared called.

A few of the kids turned to watch her. Some of them started whispering among themselves, giggling. Ariel hardly noticed. Her mind was in a very dark cloud. A thousand images flashed before her eyes—images that made bile rise in her throat. Images of Leslie and Caleb in that room, *alone*, for two weeks.

It wasn't that Ariel was jealous. Obviously not. She and Caleb weren't an item or anything. He could do whatever the hell he pleased. If he wanted to make an ass of himself, fine. It was just that he owed her an explanation for slamming the door in her face. That was all. That was why she was here. That was why she'd envisioned countless scenarios where he'd burst into the Citicorp lobby and begged her for forgiveness—where he'd insisted that he'd gone crazy and that Leslie was the biggest loser in the world. . . .

But no. No, he had to stay here with that stupid bitch. In an executive suite, no less. With a king-size bed and a whirlpool and God only knew what else.

"Slow down, will ya?" Jared begged with a nervous laugh.

Ariel came to an abrupt halt in front of the elevator.

"Um . . . are you all right?" Jared mumbled breathlessly.

"Peachy." She jabbed the button several times.

"You sure?"

She didn't answer. A bell rang, and the doors slid open. She stepped inside and punched the twentieth floor. Jared hopped in after her. The next moment they were being whisked upstairs. Ariel kept her eyes glued to passing numbers on a digital console. Four . . . five . . .

"Come *on*," she growled impatiently.

Jared cleared his throat. "You aren't mad at us or anything, are you?"

"I'm not mad at *you*," she answered.

"Are you mad at Caleb?"

Her jaw tightened. The seconds dragged on in silence—until *finally* the elevator hit the magic floor.

Once again the doors parted. Ariel stormed out into the plush hallway. A row of identical, evenly spaced doors stretched in either direction.

"Which way?" she demanded.

Jared swallowed. "End of the hall to the right," he murmured. "Number twenty-fifteen." He reached for her arm. "Ariel, why don't you tell me—"

But she just shook free. She was in no mood to talk, to pour out her *feelings*. No. She would save that for Caleb. Her face soured as she marched. The farther she got from the elevators, the more disgusting the hall became. Plates of half-eaten food and empty plastic cups were strewn across the carpet; the walls were stained with grubby handprints. And it *stank*. What was so great about this place, anyway? Even compared to the Citicorp building, the hotel was a dump.

One last door remained, emblazoned with the number 2015.

So. This is it. The "phat" room.

She paused outside and listened for a moment. Soft alternative music was playing within; she could hear quiet giggles.

Holding her breath, she banged on the door.

"It's open, baby," came the boisterous reply.

Ariel flung the door aside and stepped across the threshold.

"Ariel!" Caleb gasped. "Jeez . . ."

Her stomach turned. Caleb was sprawled across a huge, rumpled, unmade bed with Leslie and four other scantily clad girls whom Ariel had never seen before. He was turning into quite a gigolo, wasn't he? And now she saw where the stench was coming from. The entire room was covered with garbage. It looked as if they hadn't left or taken the trash out in weeks. How could they *live* like this?

"Wh-when did you get here?" Caleb stammered, fighting to sit up straight.

Ariel didn't answer. Her eyes narrowed, zeroing in on something Leslie held in her hands. It was a thick, battered book.

Ariel's heart bounced. *No way . . .*

That *book!* Could it be? But *how?* She stepped forward, just to make sure that anger and shock weren't making her totally insane—and that's when she saw the title.

Oh . . . my . . . God!

In her wildest fantasies she could never have imagined something so outrageous, so *sickening*. But the frayed, water-worn pages were unmistakable. It wasn't a copy of the same book; it was *the* one—the one that had belonged to her father: *Skintight: The Illustrated History of Erotic Film*. What the hell was Leslie doing with it?

"That's *mine!*" she shrieked. She flung out a trembling arm. "Give it to me!"

Everyone froze.

"Give it to me!" she shouted again.

Caleb shot a baffled glance at Leslie, then back at Ariel. "What are you talking about?"

"That *book*," she growled. "That book is *mine*. I lost it."

Leslie blinked at her a few times. Then she smirked. "Ahh . . . come on."

"I'm serious, dammit!"

Jared appeared at her side. "Uh . . . what's going on?" he asked fearfully.

Ariel snorted. "Leslie stole my book."

"Listen," Leslie said. She smiled sympathetically, as if Ariel were a disturbed five-year-old. "I *found* that book. It was—"

"In a black knapsack by the Snohomish River, right?" Ariel finished. "I know. That's where I lost it, along with everything else I cared about. So give it back."

Leslie's smile faded. "Okay. Somebody must have

told you about how I found it, right?" She frowned at Caleb. "Did you?"

He shook his head vehemently. "Of course not. I haven't seen her in two weeks."

Something snapped in Ariel's brain at that moment. Just the sight of this slutty girl sitting on a bed with Caleb, holding *her* book—the one thing in the world that reminded her of home, of her father—was too much to bear. She lost control. Before she was even aware of what she was doing, she dashed across the room, straight for Leslie.

"Ariel!" Caleb shouted.

One of the girls leaped from the bed and threw herself at Ariel, tackling her to the floor.

"Get off me!" Ariel snarled, shoving the girl away and rolling through the garbage. She pushed herself up and glared at her, panting. "This has nothing to do with—"

"But I *know* you," the girl interrupted.

What? Ariel frowned. Her eyes roved over the girl's shoulder-length brown hair, her green eyes, her rosy cheeks. Nope. Didn't ring a bell. But whoever she was, she had *no* taste. She was a wearing a totally ridiculous necklace—with a garish silver pendant that dangled from a silver chain down to her midriff. It looked like the pound sign on a telephone.

"I've never seen you before in my life," Ariel spat.

"I know, I know." The girl cast a frightened glance at Leslie, then turned back to Ariel. "But I've seen you. I've seen *this*. In a vision. It has something to do with the Chosen One."

Oh, please. Ariel shook her head miserably. The

need to fight suddenly drained out of her, as if a plug had been pulled in a sink. This was *exactly* what she needed right now—to meet another weirdo who babbled about the Chosen One.

"The Chosen One, huh?" Leslie hooted. "Caleb, I thought you said Ariel didn't believe in the Chosen One. No *wonder* she's so . . . you know. *Unbalanced.*"

Ariel's face darkened. "Just give me my goddamn book back, all right?"

Leslie winked at Caleb. But Caleb was just staring at Ariel as if she were a convicted criminal—with a look of unmistakable suspicion . . . and fear.

"For God's sake, Caleb!" Ariel shouted, exasperated. *"What?"*

He didn't answer.

"This is yours." The strange girl pulled off her ugly necklace, then hopped up and draped it around Ariel's neck.

"Hey!" Ariel protested. "Get this thing off of me!"

Leslie burst into laughter. But she abruptly stopped.

Because as soon as the girl let go of the necklace black welts appeared on her face. And spread to her arms. Her legs.

Within seconds she was gone.

PART III:

April 18–30

The Fourth Lunar Cycle

It was a crisp morning in late April when Naamah arrived at the Promised Land.

She was very pleased to see how much progress Harold Wurf had made in such a short time. He was obviously an intelligent boy. He was stripping his followers of their former identities—forcing them to toil in the fields, forcing them to wear the same white garb. And as they gazed upon his commandments he was slowly and subtly destroying their free will.

All in all, a job well done.

But not even Harold's wily tactics and megalomania would be enough to convert the Visionaries. That was why he needed the Demon's help.

He would never know the truth, of course. He'd never know his Promised Land had been infiltrated. No—Harold Wurf would believe that the miracles of the coming months would be of his own doing. He truly believed that he was a savior. Naamah's hand would remain unseen. And the Visionaries would descend upon this place, searching for their Chosen One. . . .

Some of them would be easily converted and eliminated. Their visions were weak; their minds were weaker.

Others would prove more difficult.

But Naamah was supremely confident. Every Prophecy had been fulfilled thus far. And any human being—no matter how strong—could be manipulated. That was a lesson Naamah had learned long ago. She had plenty of time. Her stay among Harold's flock would be an extended one.

Besides, nobody would suspect any foul play. The scroll had surely been destroyed in the floods. No one could ever know that a false prophet would lead the Visionaries astray. And all the while the Chosen One would remain at a safe distance—helpless and unaware.

Lilith herself would tend to that.

So Naamah marched up to the farmhouse and presented herself to the Healer. She armed herself with an appropriately nondescript alias: From this moment forward she was Linda Altman, the orphaned Brit—stranded in the United States, plagued by visions, adrift and alone. . . .

Yet she could finally rejoice. She'd found Harold

Wurf, the true Chosen One. She'd seen his face in her visions. The magic fires across the countryside had pointed the way.

And she had a secret, too.

There were some confused souls among Harold's flock. There were Visionaries in the Promised Land who weren't convinced of his legitimacy. Some dark force was at work—clouding their minds, poisoning their hearts. These Visionaries knew of the Chosen One . . . but they didn't think he was Dr. Harold Wurf.

Harold had to prove himself again.

But Harold promised Linda Altman there was nothing to fear. Nobody could pose any threat to him. He gave her his word. . . .

Naamah was surprised at how easily she slipped into the role of a subservient follower.

True, she served the Demon—but she was a leader among the Lilum. She was the warrior-priestess, the magician who carried out the Demon's will on earth. But she was also a chameleon . . . much like Lilith herself. Different situations demanded different faces. She could be anything to anyone at any time.

It was the key to her power.

Amarillo, Texas
Night of April 20

"I brought you here tonight to answer your questions," the voice of Dr. Harold Wurf boomed over a hidden loudspeaker. "I brought you here to allay your fears and to tell you my story."

It's about time, George thought angrily. He fidgeted on the hard seat of the wooden folding chair, glancing around at the other kids in the candlelit barn. There were thirteen altogether, including him and Julia—sitting in a circle. In a *circle*. How lame was that? It made him feel as if he were in kindergarten or something. And nobody else seemed to like it, either. They all looked as uncomfortable and pissed off as *he* did.

"Are you all right?" Julia whispered beside him. She squeezed his hand.

George shrugged. "I guess," he muttered. But he wasn't. For starters, it reeked of cow manure. The candles were making him kind of edgy because the floor was covered with straw. If one of the candles tipped, the whole place would go up in a second. But maybe that was what Harold wanted. Maybe he just planned on getting rid of George and all the rest of them, human barbecue style. Anything was possible. After all, those

97

girls in Jackson wanted to kill him, right? It wouldn't be a big shocker if this guy wanted him dead, too.

"I'd like to begin by welcoming you again to the Promised Land," Harold continued. "Destiny has brought you here. You are the special ones. You've had visions. You've heard the name of the Chosen One. Your powers have drawn you to this place. . . ."

Wrong. George ended up at this place totally by accident. He was *trying* to go west. He would have kept going, too . . . if it weren't for those fires. And for Julia. For some reason, she couldn't bring herself to leave. She kept saying she needed to find out more about Harold. More what? They'd been here ten days already. Ten days too long, as far as George was concerned. All they did was sit around and eat undercooked corn and argue about whether *this* was the place or not. Of course it wasn't! Why couldn't Julia *see* that? She still had visions; she still felt the pull west, didn't she? So what was the deal?

". . . but to live in the Promised Land, you must abide by my commandments," Harold concluded. "Now you may ask your questions."

"I got a question," George snapped. "Where the hell *are* you?"

"My duties require me to be many places at once," the voice answered.

Nice one, George thought. This dude must have been a con artist before the plague. He was probably a convict, too. Yeah. George knew the type. There were dozens of them back in Pittsburgh: smooth-talking, good-looking slimeballs who could make a sucker out of almost anyone. George had to hand it to the guy . . . it looked as if the chumps in this barn were starting to fall for his act. They were all avoiding George's eyes, shifting awkwardly in their chairs.

He stole a quick peek at Julia. Her face was blank. Was she falling for it, too?

"Any other questions?" Harold asked.

"Yeah, I got another," George called. "What's up with the white dresses? Why does everybody gotta wear 'em? Is it a rule? 'Cause it isn't painted on that tower."

There was a pause. George could feel Julia glaring at him.

Hmmm. Maybe he should lighten up a little. No . . . if she was mad, that was *her* problem. *Somebody* had to step up to this guy.

"The clothing of the Promised Land symbolizes many things," Harold finally stated. "The shedding of old ways. The donning of new ways. The severing of all previous ties—to family, country, culture, and religion. In the Promised Land we begin a new life. We are all equal. We are all the same. We wear white because white is every color bled into one."

Oh, brother. George almost laughed. What kind of garbage was *that?* Harold sounded as if he were ripping off lyrics from a really bad seventies rock song.

"White ain't *my* color, buddy," he yelled with a grin. "You got anything in fuscia?"

"*George!*" Julia snapped.

"Do you doubt me, George?" Harold asked. "Because—" He broke off.

99

There were some mutterings, then a screech of feedback.

Everybody in the room winced.

"I'm sorry," Harold apologized after a moment. "I must leave you now. One of my flock has taken ill. I'll return as soon as I can."

The loudspeaker clicked and fell silent.

George rolled his eyes. "So much for hearing his story," he mumbled. He stood and shook his head. "Come on, Julia. This whole thing is a crock—"

"Why do you mock him?" a girl from the circle interrupted.

Whoa.

George did a double take, caught off guard by the girl's accent. She sounded British. But she sure as hell looked American. For chrissakes, she was wearing a black sweatshirt with the word *Graceland* written in silver glitter. Actually, she looked like a cheerleader— with long blond curls and bright blue eyes and a perfect apple-pie face. In short, she looked like the kind of upstanding, straight-arrow type who used to make George sick.

"You're not from around here, are you?" he asked.

Julia reached up and tugged at his T-shirt. "George, come on," she whispered. "Don't be rude. Just sit down. . . ."

"No, it's all right," the girl insisted. She smiled at Julia, then glanced back up at George. "No, I'm not from around here. I'm from Manchester, England."

"England?" George frowned. "How did you get *here?*"

"By accident, really." She lowered her eyes. "My family wanted to spend Christmas holiday driving across the States. . . ." She looked up at him again. "But it doesn't matter. What matters is that we're all here now. And this Healer is our only hope."

"Our only hope," George repeated, but he softened his tone. He slumped back into the chair. "Look. I don't know about *England*—but here in the USA we got a word for what this dude Wurf is trying to pull. It's called a *scam.*" He carefully enunciated the last word. "Get it?"

The girl smiled. "Yeah, I get it," she said dryly. "And in England we have a word when we've heard enough from little wankers like you. *Bollocks.*"

George blinked.

Then he cracked up. Surprise, surprise. This girl was sharper than he thought. He shot a brief glance at Julia. She was shaking her head with a serves-you-right smirk on her face.

"I like that word," he remarked, turning back to the girl. "What's your name?"

"Linda," she replied. She eyed him coolly. "What's yours?"

"George." He nodded. "You're a funny girl, Linda."

She cocked her eyebrow. "Well, it's not hard to make Americans laugh. Anything vulgar does the trick."

He smiled. She really *was* sharp. "You're right. But if you're so smart, explain something to me. Why can't you see Harold's bull for what it is?"

Linda's face grew serious. She leaned forward in her chair. "I *do* see, George," she stated quietly. "I've seen for a long time now—even before I arrived here. And believe me, it's not *bull,* as you say."

George's eyes narrowed. "What do you mean, you've seen for a long time?"

"In *visions,* George." She waved her hand around the circle. "You heard the Healer. We're all Visionaries in this room. He brought us here together for a *reason.*"

Some of the kids began to nod.

George looked at Julia again. She shrugged, as if to say: *Maybe you should listen up.*

"You saw Harold in your visions?" he asked Linda. "You actually saw his face?"

"I wouldn't be here if I didn't," she replied. She was clearly dead serious.

George glanced at some of the others. "What about the rest of you?" he asked. "Have *you* seen Harold?"

A few people shook their heads. Some of them looked at each other. They all looked as though they were waiting for somebody else to speak first.

"Well, *I* haven't seen Harold," George stated in the silence. "All I see is myself, doing something weird that I don't understand. And I know about the Chosen One, but I don't know who she is. But I *do* know that she's a chick." *Oops.* That might have offended somebody. "I mean, a *female,*" he quickly added.

One of the kids—a wimpy-looking guy with droopy brown eyes—cleared his throat. "Yeah, that's what I think, too. I don't know why, though."

"Me too," a girl piped in.

Pretty soon everybody except Linda was nodding in agreement.

George lifted his shoulders. "How do you explain that?"

"I can't," Linda said. "But I have a theory. Do you know about . . . the Demon?"

The Demon. Yeah, George knew about the Demon. But he was kind of hoping nobody would bring it up. Just hearing the word made him all tense. He didn't want to talk about it.

"I think that the Demon is close by," Linda continued. "Closer than we think. I think the Demon is *here* on earth. Maybe even in this country."

"I do, too," Julia agreed softly.

"Me too," the wimpy-looking kid said. "I *know* that the Demon is here. And I know that she's a girl. Like us. I've had a vision where I can almost see her, but she puts a blindfold over me. . . ."

George hesitated. He scratched at his stringy blond hair. He knew exactly what they were talking about. All of them. In his visions he could almost *feel* the Demon beside him. But what did that have to do with Harold's being a scam artist?

"So?" he finally asked.

Linda gazed at him. "I think that the Demon is trying to confuse us, George. Or worse."

"What do you mean?" he demanded.

She drummed her fingernails on her knees. "Look, I wasn't going to mention this, but something happened to me before I got here. In Tennessee. It was pouring rain, and I had to find shelter. So I ended up at an old house that was filled with girls. They asked me if I had visions. I said yes. You see, before I met them, I thought I was going crazy. I didn't know that other people saw things. I was so relieved to talk about it that I admitted everything to them. I told them about the Chosen One. About the things I saw."

George swallowed. A bizarre sensation gripped him: He felt as if he were having an extended attack of déjà vu, an attack that wouldn't end. It was as if he could predict every word that came out of her mouth. . . .

"They tried to kill you, didn't they?" he whispered.

"Yes." She lowered her eyes for a moment, staring down at her lap. "I had to defend myself." Her face grew pained. "It was . . . it was bad." She looked up again. "But I think those girls might be connected with the Demon."

George nodded. "You're probably right. But that has nothing to do with Harold. I mean—what if *Harold* is connected to the Demon, too? What if *you're* the one who's confused?" He reached over and took Julia's hand. "The same thing happened to me and her. We found a house full of sick girls, too. And we learned something. You can't trust *anybody*. You can't stay in one place. Especially now, if the Demon is here on earth. You have to keep moving."

Linda shook her head. "We *can't*, though!" she cried. "What about these fires? They block all the roads except the roads that lead here. How do you explain that?"

"I . . ." He slouched back in his seat. "I can't. But—"

"I can't, either," Linda stated. "But you know what? I think that they're like a maze—a maze that leads to the Chosen One. Believe me, if I thought Harold was a fraud or dangerous, I'd be the first to leave. But we're *safe* here, George." Her voice rose. She straightened, sitting on the edge of her seat.

"Nobody's trying to hurt us. Harold *wants* us to talk about our visions. He feeds us. He doesn't make us do anything we don't want to. Everybody here has seen him perform miracles. And if we leave, what's to prevent us from running into those girls again?"

George stared back at her. He wanted to argue . . . but he couldn't. Everything she said was true. Even if it was boring here, it *was* safe. Out in the rest of the world, it wasn't. He *knew* that. He'd almost been killed more than once.

And if the Demon were close, he'd probably stand a better chance of survival with a *group* of kids than on his own. At least he hoped he would. But the fact was, he knew nothing about the Demon—other than that she was more powerful than anyone or anything he'd ever seen.

That was the scariest thing of all.

"She's right, George," Julia murmured, gently caressing his hand.

"I know," he murmured. He turned to her, gazing into those beautiful brown eyes. It was clear that *she* wanted to stay. And in the end, she was his first priority. She was all that mattered. Maybe he should just suck it up and give the place another shot. . . .

There wouldn't be any harm in staying a little while longer, would there?

Seattle, Washington
Early morning of April 26

Ariel yawned. She lay on her back. Her eyes were closed. She felt deliciously warm both inside and out. The anger, the pain, the loneliness—all of it had disappeared like a bad dream. She even managed to forget about the weird girl who vaporized right in front of her, about Leslie and *Skintight* . . . about Caleb and the fact that he still hadn't apologized. Well, almost, anyway.

How many nights had she drunk herself to sleep? It didn't matter. The drowsy sound of a crackling fire filled her ears. The flames were so close, so snuggly, like an invisible blanket. She had a fleeting thought of Brian . . . on a bus somewhere with a bunch of wacked-out strangers. He must be miserable.

Wrong move, Bri, she told him with a grin. *You should have stayed with me—*

"Hey, Ariel! Ariel! Get out of there!"

Her nose wrinkled. A girl was screaming at her from miles away.

"You hear me? Get out!"

For a moment she wondered: *Is that girl's voice in my head?* It sounded too crazed and distant to be real.

"Can you hear me? *Get out!*"

Of course I can hear you, Ariel thought, frowning.

"Hey! Hey!"

She sighed. If that girl . . .

Something hot and unpleasant flowed into Ariel's lungs. She coughed once. Then she coughed again. *That* was strange. She was having a hard time catching her breath. Red patterns swirled under her eyelids. Her brain felt like a balloon, slowly rising off the floor. Maybe she should take a peek at what was going on. She wanted to open her eyes, *really*—but she just couldn't muster the energy. Oh, well.

"Come on! Get up!"

Something crashed and tinkled. It sounded like glass. But the noise was so faint, just like the girl's voice. Had somebody thrown a rock through a window? Why? All right. Something really weird was going on here. But she couldn't understand it; her mind was so scattered. Up and up she floated—straight into the shifting sea of red.

It was *hot* in here. Really hot.

Where *was* she, anyway? Was she back in the Citicorp lobby? She thought she ended up crashing in the conference room of the hotel, but she could have been wrong.

Once more thick heat stabbed into her chest. She coughed again. She was choking. Fear scuttled at the edge of her mind. But her eyes remained closed, as if they were disconnected from the rest of her body.

There was another sound: the pattering of approaching feet.

"Damn," a voice muttered above her.

Pointy little fingers started tickling Ariel's back. Her fear drifted away, forgotten. She almost giggled. Her body rocked back and forth a few times, then—*whoops!*—she was being hoisted into the air, lifted away from that wonderful heat. . . . Something was holding her up. Her body bounced along unsteadily, lurching back and forth. Wind whipped at her face. She shivered. Was she going to fall?

Plop.

Yeah, she was. She dropped right into something soft, cold, and wet. Her butt was suddenly chilled. Enough was enough. She had to find out what was happening.

But then a pair of sloppy wet lips smothered her own.

Jesus!

Hot breath filled her mouth. It tasted like tomatoes and clams. *No, no*—somebody was trying to *kiss* her! Rage surged through her veins. The next thing she knew, she was viciously shoving her hands into a flat, taut stomach. "Yeecch!" she spluttered. She blinked and spit a few times, trying to rid herself of that foul, salty flavor. She was livid. Of all the disgusting things . . .

"Are you all right?" a familiar, breathless voice asked.

Ariel's eyes snapped open. She *knew* that voice—

"Leslie?" she shrieked.

It was Leslie. *Leslie!* **Ariel shuddered, over-**whelmed with revulsion. What in God's name was Leslie *thinking?* Ariel knew the girl was weird, but she never once figured . . . She cringed, unable to complete the thought. She felt *violated.*

"Are you all right?" Leslie repeated. She was panting. Her face was sweaty. Her curls hung over her shoulders in damp disarray.

"No, I'm not all right!" Ariel barked. "Don't *touch* me! If you touch me again, I swear to God, I'll *kill* you!"

Leslie just shook her head. Then of all things, she *smiled.*

As Ariel continued to glare at the girl she noticed something peculiar: Leslie's olive skin was lit with a flickering orange light.

Wait a second. Ariel was *way* too disoriented. There was a haze in the air. The sun was shining. When had the sun come up? As far as she knew, it was the middle of the night. . . . It took her a few more moments to realize that she was sitting on a damp lawn on a downtown Seattle street, surrounded by skyscrapers—and that kids were screaming and running all around her. What the hell was going on?

"Do you know what I just did?" Leslie asked with a smirk.

Ariel's eyes narrowed. *What you just did? Yeah. You tried to kiss me, you freak.*

"Look behind you," Leslie instructed. "Go ahead."

For some reason, Ariel found she couldn't

move. If Leslie was playing some kind of perverted joke, it wasn't funny. Not at all. Not only was Leslie pissing her off, but she was freaking her out as well. Majorly.

"Whatever," Leslie mumbled. She rolled her eyes and pushed herself to her feet, keeping her gaze fixed on a spot above Ariel's head. "By the way, you're welcome."

Finally Ariel mustered the courage to glance over her shoulder.

No. No way . . .

She saw nothing but fire.

The first six floors of the Sheraton Seattle Hotel were engulfed in flame. Thick black smoke poured from broken windows, filling the street with a dank, poisonous-smelling fog. Ariel gasped. She started breathing heavily. The place had become an inferno—and she'd almost slept right through it.

"Just so you know, kissing girls isn't my thing," Leslie stated dryly. "I was giving you mouth-to-mouth. I like guys, thank you very much."

Ariel turned back to Leslie, her mouth agape. She had no idea how to respond to that, to what was happening. Her brain stewed with a dozen different emotions: fear, confusion, embarrassment, indignation . . . but she was too baffled and frightened to make sense of it all.

"What a bummer," Leslie grumbled, staring at the blaze. "I was really starting to dig that place." She sighed, then laughed. "But hey, whatcha gonna do? You know how the song goes." She sang in a jokey, high-pitched voice: *"'Nothing lasts forever but the earth and sky. . . .'"*

Ariel tried to swallow. The words drifted right past her. She couldn't stop staring at Leslie. "You . . . you got me out of there?" she croaked.

Leslie shrugged. "What can I say? I love your necklace. I couldn't exactly let that fine piece of jewelry go to waste, now, could I?"

Ariel blinked a few times. She glanced down at herself. The ugly silver pendant hung from her neck. *What the hell?* There must have been a reason why she hadn't taken it off . . . but what was it? Something about wanting to prove to Leslie and Caleb that it was important to respect the dead, even weirdos like that girl—

"Just kidding," Leslie said. She shot Ariel a quick smile. "You know, you're heavier than you look. Ever thought about Ultra Slim-Fast?"

Ultra Slim-Fast. Ariel shook her head. None of Leslie's words seemed to make any sense. Ariel was fast slipping into a state of uncomprehending shock. Had Leslie just saved her *life?* Was that possible? She opened her mouth to demand an explanation—but Leslie's expression abruptly changed.

The humor was gone. Horror took its place.

Without warning, Leslie bolted past Ariel toward the building.

Ariel whirled around. "Wait!" she shrieked. "What's happening?"

But Leslie didn't reply. She kept running, straight at the flames, staring at a window on the fifth floor. It suddenly burst into pieces, releasing a torrent of smoke. Ariel gazed up at it, transfixed. Her breathing grew more labored. Two arms flopped over the windowsill—and the next moment a long-haired body tumbled into the air, hurtling to the pavement in front of the revolving doors. It landed with a thump.

Bile rose in Ariel's throat. Even through all the smoke and people everywhere she could see the blood. . . .

Leslie dashed to the body and fell to her knees.

"Jared!" she shouted, scooping him into her arms. "Jared! Can you hear me?"

Jared? Ariel's heart plummeted. She hadn't even recognized him. But it was Jared, all right—she could see it now: his scruff, his clownish face. Caleb's best friend. *Her* friend.

And he was most certainly dead.

At that moment everything snapped into focus.

She would be dead if it weren't for Leslie.

"Caleb!" Leslie started screaming. She clung to Jared's limp body, feverishly looking in all directions, her matted black hair spinning like helicopter blades around her head. "Caleb, come here!"

Ariel choked for air. *Oh, no.* Was Caleb still in there? She was practically hyperventilating. . . . She struggled to push herself to her feet—but her head seemed to swoop into a cloud of purplish haze, and she immediately collapsed back to her knees.

"Caleb!" Leslie shouted again.

A lone figure dashed out of the smoke. *Thank God!* Even in her semidelirious state Ariel could

113

see that it was Caleb, alive. . . . His hair flew behind his back as he sprinted over to Leslie. He grabbed her shoulders and gently pulled her away from Jared's body.

"Wait!" Ariel croaked desperately. "Over here!"

"Ariel?" Caleb's head snapped in her direction. He staggered across the lawn, dragging Leslie with him. Ariel breathed a sigh of relief.

"We gotta get out of here," Caleb muttered, crouching beside her. "The entire city's going up."

Leslie stared at him.

For once—much to Ariel's amazement—she looked scared.

"What's happening?" Leslie asked. "What started it?"

Caleb shook his head. "Beats the hell out of me." His eyes flashed between the two of them. "But we gotta split. *Now.*"

Ariel nodded. "I . . . I know where we can go," she found herself saying. "It's not far. About thirty miles. We can be there in a few days."

"Where?" Caleb and Leslie both demanded at once.

Back to where I started. She hadn't been one hundred percent sure until this very moment . . . but she knew where she had to go.

Babylon.

It was time to face Trevor. He *was* her brother. In a way, he was all she had left. There was nothing for her *here*—Seattle was rapidly turning into a pile of cinders. Maybe Trevor had changed in these past few months. Maybe he would apologize. And despite the fact that

114

Jezebel had betrayed her, she'd also once told Ariel that they were family. She'd meant it, too. She'd been drunk. People always told the truth when they were drunk.

"Where, Ariel?" Caleb repeated.

She took a deep breath. "Home," she said.

ELEVEN

Carnival cruise ship *The Majestic,*
near Crete
Morning of April 28

*"Death will court her—tempting her with its dark
sleep. . . ."*

Sarah crouched on the cold metal floor, gazing
down at the scroll. A tear fell from her cheek. She
didn't even notice until it splattered softly on the yel-
low parchment and smudged some of the tiny letters.

How many hours had she been stuck on this one
line?

She didn't know. She only knew that it had never
seemed more *accurate,* more *personal.* Death was in-
deed tempting. Death would put an end to the agony,
a stop to the pain that throbbed within every exhausted bone of her malnourished body. Death would
take her out of the stink of this cramped cell—where
the lights blazed incessantly, where the division between day and night had no meaning, where she'd
been stuffed like trash with a hundred other pitiful
kids who'd offended the soldiers or lost the lottery. . . .

Am I the Chosen One? she screamed silently at
the text. *Am I? Answer me!*

But it wouldn't. And that was the greatest torture
of all. She still needed that one final bit of proof.

117

That one irrefutable piece of evidence. A final miracle to confirm beyond any doubt that *Sarah Levy* was the Chosen One. Because if she *weren't,* if she were just another teenager . . . then she could die in peace. The burden would be lifted. It wouldn't make a single bit of difference if her life came to an end.

"Qu'est-ce que c'est?" a harsh voice barked next to her.

Sarah winced. She glanced up from the parchment.

A sickly boy with dark eyes was leering at her. He jerked a finger at the scroll. *"Ça. Cette chose. Qu'est-ce que c'est?"*

"I . . . I don't speak French," Sarah murmured.

His lips curled contemptuously. *"Tu es américaine, non?"*

She swallowed. There was something unbalanced in his face—something desperate and dangerous. A thought occurred to her: He could leap out and strangle her, and she wouldn't be able to do a thing about it. They were locked behind a bolted steel door. She couldn't scream for help, either. The soldiers ignored the cries that came from this place.

Her eyes flashed over the rest of the prisoners, sprawled in tatters across the floor, muttering quietly among themselves. Would anybody here help her?

Probably not.

A chill ran down her spine. *This must be how slaves felt,* she thought. *Packed together like cattle, stripped of their dignity, unable to communicate . . . without hope. And soon we're going to be tossed overboard in some strange country where we're all going to die. We'll never get back to America, back to*

118

civilization. I'll never see Mom and Dad again.

"Bête," the boy suddenly spat. He shambled away from her.

Sarah hung her head. She sighed—and the next thing she knew, she was bawling uncontrollably.

What's happening to me?

Huge sobs racked her weakened frame. She used to be so strong, so sure of herself. Even when her body was suffering, her mind was clear.

Not anymore.

Sniffing, she turned back to the scroll. The prophecies almost seemed to mock her now: *"A false prophet will arise in the New World. . . ."*

The New World probably meant America. But Sarah would never find out. She'd never make it home. She'd never know if that girl Aviva was right . . . if the disease hadn't struck there, if her parents were still alive. And she'd never be able to warn anyone about this false prophet—whoever he or she was.

". . . the Demon assumes a human form, walking among the righteous and the wicked."

She shivered, wiping the tears from her eyes.

She couldn't warn anyone about the Demon, either. Nobody would know that the Demon was coming. Fear gripped her—and the fear turned to terror. What did that *mean,* assuming a human form? Did it mean that the Demon would possess somebody? Did it mean that the Demon would invade the body of some unsuspecting person—or maybe even somebody who was willing?

Who was this Demon, this enemy of the Chosen One?

It was just one of a thousand questions and riddles that would go unanswered.

Her only hope—her *only* hope—was to crack the code.

But as for that . . . well, she didn't even know where to *start*. Okay, that wasn't quite true; she figured that the code probably had something to do with the little passages of nonsense words. Why *else* would they be there? She also figured that the dates might play a role in cracking it since they were included in those passages and not in the main text. *How* still remained an utter mystery. Besides, even when she was fit and healthy and happy, she stunk at mathematical puzzles. Josh was the math and science whiz. She'd barely passed algebra.

Uh-oh.

That French boy was staring at her again.

He took two steps toward her, then paused and scowled at the bolted door.

"Écoutez!" he yelled. *"Tout le monde, écoutez!"*

A hush fell over the room.

Sarah glanced at the door, then back at him. Her stomach squeezed.

What did he *want?* Was he talking to *her?*

Wait. There was a sound outside in the hall . . . the sound of scuffling feet. *Oh, God.* Maybe he'd succeeded in summoning the guards. Maybe he was going to accuse her of something. Maybe the guards were just going to toss her overboard—

The latch turned. Sarah held her breath. The thick steel door swung open with a metallic squeal. . . .

"Sarah?"

Ibrahim! Her legs nearly gave out from under her.

His head poked into the room—only his head. He looked terrified. His eyes were wide and his nose was dripping with sweat.

"Come on!" he whispered. "Get out of there!"

A hidden reserve of energy seemed to unleash itself. Sarah snatched up the scroll and bolted through the doorway. The French boy shouted something at her—but was instantly silenced when Ibrahim slammed the door behind them.

"We don't have much time," Ibrahim whispered, glancing in either direction down the dark, narrow corridor. He held a shiny gold key in one hand.

"What's going on?" Sarah breathed. Her heart was beating so fast, she could hardly talk.

"Aviva stole the master key from one of the guards," he said quietly.

"Aviva?" she gasped.

He nodded, squeezing her against him. He started dragging her to the left, toward a closed cabin door. "She sees things, too, Sarah. She has visions. She knows about the Chosen One. And she says that the Demon is coming. The Demon is going to appear very soon. Within days."

"I . . . I don't understand," Sarah stammered, struggling as best she could to keep up with him. "How does she—"

"Keep quiet," he interrupted. "I'll explain everything later. Right now I have to hide you and get this key back to the guard before he notices it's missing."

Sarah bit her tongue. So this was a breakout. That

was all she needed to know. If she wanted it to work, she would keep her mouth shut.

"In here," he muttered.

He paused outside the door and tried to jab the key into the lock. But his hands were shaking too much. He couldn't get it to fit. . . .

"Arrêtez!"

Ibrahim's hand froze.

Oh, no. Sarah stifled a scream. *No—*

"Or should we say 'stop'?" a cruelly familiar British voice chimed in. "You two *do* speak English after all."

A pair of heavy footsteps clomped down the hall.

Sarah swiveled around.

Not them!

The footsteps belonged to the fat French soldier and the British soldier who'd clobbered Ibrahim. Both had their machine guns drawn. Sarah slumped against the door, unable to support her own weight anymore. Fear robbed her of any remaining strength.

"Well, what have we here?" the British soldier asked, stopping short about five paces from her. He raised the gun to his eyes and peered down the sights, aiming the barrel directly at her chest. "A little unscheduled stroll about the ship?"

Ibrahim stepped forward, clasping his hands. "Please," he pleaded. His voice quavered. "We don't mean any harm. We don't want to cause any trouble. But you left us with no choice. This is a very special girl. You have to understand that—"

"A special girl?" He laughed once, then glanced at the French soldier. *"Tu comprends? Elle est une fille . . . speciale."* He lingered on the last word.

The French soldier snickered.

Sarah gulped painfully. Her grip tightened around the scroll's pegs. She couldn't tear her eyes from that gun. If he moved his finger the slightest amount, she'd be dead. Instantly.

"Why don't you explain to us how special she is," the British soldier murmured, turning his attention back to Sarah. "I'd really like to know."

"She was sent here to end the plague," Ibrahim stated.

Sarah's jaw dropped. *What?* Where on earth had Ibrahim come up with *that?*

The British soldier lowered his gun for a moment. "Sent here, eh?" He grinned. His brow grew furrowed. "By whom, exactly?"

"It's all—it's all in that scroll," Ibrahim stuttered. "Believe me. It prophesied that she would come. It prophesied when the rains would end. It talks of powers and—"

"Thank you," the soldier cut in. "That's quite enough." He shot a hard glance at Sarah. "Let's hear from you now. You say you were sent here to stop the plague?"

Sarah shook her head. "I . . . I . . . no, but you see—"

"*No?*" he interrupted sarcastically. "But your friend here says you are. He claims it's in that scroll." He shifted his gun to one hand and stepped forward, his arm outstretched. "Here, allow me. Perhaps I can find it."

Instinctively Sarah flinched, clutching the scroll against her.

"Allons-y," the French soldier muttered. *"Vite."*

The British soldier nodded. He took a deep breath, then withdrew his arm and dug his hand into a baggy pocket on his fatigues. "Very well," he stated. He fished out a short metal baton with a switch on it. "This scroll is rubbish. *The Majestic*'s policy is to burn rubbish."

He flicked the switch with his thumb.

A bright, pinkish flame leaped from the end of the baton.

"No!" Sarah cried. She cowered against the door, squeezing the scroll with every remaining ounce of strength. The flame burned very violently and loudly, sending a shower of sparks into the air. "You can't! Don't—"

"Of course we can," the soldier interrupted. "This is only a flare, but it will do quite nicely."

I won't let this happen. . . .

Panicked, Sarah bolted down the hall. But the British soldier kicked out his leg—striking her shins and sending her tumbling face first to the floor. Her knees and palms struck the metal with a painful smack.

The scroll clattered away from her.

"No!" she shrieked. She tried to claw her way after it. "No—"

"Tais-toi!" the French soldier snapped, shoving the tip of his gun against her nose.

Blood turned to ice in Sarah's veins.

Very calmly and deliberately, the British soldier strolled over to the scroll and bent down beside it. "Cheers," he said. He touched the flame to the parchment.

The next instant the scroll was alive with fire.

Sarah's mouth opened in a silent scream.

Idiots! Don't you understand what you're doing? Don't you— Her eyes widened.

Wait.

Something very strange was happening.

The scroll was burning . . . but it *wasn't.*

She blinked. The parchment didn't blacken or curl or turn to ash. Even the wooden pegs remained totally unscathed. Her heart skipped a beat. She could still see the scrawl of letters through the blaze. Nothing was being consumed. *Nothing.* How was that *possible?* A peculiar terror washed over her. The fire grew more intense, crackling with a tremendous fury . . . until all at once the flames leaped into the air and vanished in a cloud of smoke.

But the scroll still lay on the floor—unblemished, as if it had never been touched.

TWELVE

Washington Institute of Technology
Babylon, Washington
Afternoon of April 27

There was fear in the boy's eyes. Trevor Collins could see it.

"Why are you *doing* this to me?" the boy pleaded. "Please let me go. Please. I can't be in here anymore. Okay? I *mean* it."

Trevor was grateful for the thick metal door and the small window of shatterproof glass that stood between them. Not that this boy seemed particularly violent. But Trevor knew that even the most docile of the mentally ill could become . . . unpredictable.

"Lemme *out!*" the boy shrieked. He began pacing around the sterile classroom in tight circles. He rubbed his arms through the sleeves of his pajamas. "Don't you see? You can't *do* this! I *see* things! The Chosen One needs me. I know it. Doesn't that *mean* anything to you?"

You're just making it harder on yourself, Trevor silently admonished. He brushed a strand of blondish brown hair out of his eyes.

"You're sick!" the boy hissed at him. "You're a sick bastard!"

Ah, yes . . . the wondrous effects of panic. Once

127

the name-calling started, a rampage inevitably followed. And then—well, it wouldn't be long. Trevor glanced down at his digital watch. The boy had been confined for exactly five hours, forty-three minutes, and eighteen seconds. Not bad. He was doing a lot better than the last subject, in fact. *That poor girl.* She had succumbed to hysteria after only an hour. She vaporized less than fifteen minutes later.

"I've gotta get to the river," the boy muttered. He stepped toward the door, glaring at Trevor through the tiny window. "The Chosen One *needs* me to go to the river."

Trevor shook his head. *The Chosen One.* Even after all this time he was still amazed by this mass delusion, this bizarre phenomenon that afflicted so many kids—Chosen One syndrome, as he'd come to call it. Every case was different. But the pattern was always the same: The deluded kids would talk of visions—and then, suddenly, they would feel compelled to perform a task on behalf of this "Chosen One." Often the task was quite trivial. But if prevented, the subjects would vaporize. If allowed to fulfill their paranoid fantasies, they would bolt from the premises, never to be seen again.

Incredible.

Of course, that was *all* he knew—even after three whole months of careful scientific study. He was still no closer to figuring out what *caused* COS. Or what caused the plague, for that matter. He was still no closer to finding a cure. And although he was certain that the two diseases were connected, he didn't know how. So he could only continue to observe, to experiment, while the clock ticked inexorably toward his own twenty-first birthday. . . .

At least there was no shortage of subjects. Another victim of COS seemed to stumble onto campus every day. It was almost as if they were drawn to the place. But why wouldn't they be? Trevor was running the only self-contained, self-sufficient, crime-free, drug-free society in the history of the world—before *or* after the plague. The first real utopia. A paradise amidst the chaos. Somebody must have spread rumors about it. . . .

"Trevor?" a voice called from the end of the hall.

"What is it?" he demanded, keeping his eyes fixed on the window.

"I . . . uh, think you better come here."

Trevor frowned. He knew the voice well. It belonged to Barney—a trusted member of his security detail, a former classmate at engineering school. Barney knew better than to disturb Trevor during an experiment.

"I'm busy," Trevor stated flatly.

"It's your girlfriend."

Trevor shot Barney a cold stare. "What about her?"

Barney stood in the open doorway, shaking his head. His pasty, rodentlike face was creased with worry. "You better take a look for yourself. She's . . . um, she's in one of the dorm rooms. She isn't feeling well."

Feeling well? Trevor grimaced. What else was new? Jezebel Howe never felt well. She was always complaining of *some* ailment—a cold, a headache, whatever. He strode down the hall. "This better be important," he grumbled. "That boy could vaporize at any minute."

Barney stepped aside as Trevor approached. "I'll keep an eye on him in the monitor. If he starts to—"

"Did she ask for help?" Trevor interrupted impatiently. He marched through the door into a vast, buzzing room. His footsteps fell silent on the smooth carpet. The only light came from the flickering blue glow of television sets . . . eighty of them in all, stacked along the wall in five neat, square grids of sixteen.

A dozen kids stood at attention—his closest friends. They were all armed with rifles. Like Barney, they'd helped him build this place. He could trust them with anything.

"Well?" he pressed. "Did she?"

"Not in so many words," Barney replied, following close behind him.

Trevor's eyes slowly roved over the sea of screens, seeking out Jezebel's mane of long black hair. In spite of his displeasure at being interrupted, he *did* enjoy coming here. It represented his greatest achievement. If it weren't for this place, he wouldn't be able to maintain the strict discipline that allowed the campus to work so beautifully.

From here he and his friends could monitor everybody else at all times. He'd rigged every single room in each of the three working buildings with a video camera—even the bathrooms and closets. It had taken weeks of work, miles of extension cable, and countless trips to and from the electronics warehouse at Old Pine Mall . . . but it had been well worth the effort.

Because now, for all intents and purposes, WIT was a giant *Real World*.

And everybody knew that Trevor and his friends were watching. Twenty-four hours a day. Seven days a week.

"There she is," Barney said. He pointed to a screen in the bottom-left corner of the center grid. "See what I mean?"

Trevor crouched beside the television set. His brow grew furrowed. *Wow.* Something *was* wrong with Jezebel. She was rolling around on a bed—in just a bra and underpants. And she was pulling at her hair and yelling something. Her skin seemed even paler than usual. It was the color of bone. . . .

"How long has this been going on?" Trevor asked worriedly.

"I noticed it about ten minutes ago," Barney replied.

Could this be COS? No—not Jezebel. She would have exhibited the symptoms long ago. Trevor leaned forward and pressed his finger against the volume button. Gradually her squeaky voice swelled in the TV's little speaker.

". . . and I know you're in there watching me," she jabbered. "You and all your sick buddies. But you're not watching *me* anymore, you see." She burst into laughter, then whirled to face the camera. "You're watching someone else! Someone you can't even begin to understand!"

Trevor flinched. What the hell was going on? He licked his lips nervously. Had she somehow gotten ahold of some drugs? She must have. But how? It was impossible—Trevor had drug dealers shot on sight. No one would dare smuggle drugs into the campus.

The only other possible explanation was that she was having some kind of mental breakdown. *No, no.* After all the years spent pining after this girl, after convincing her to stay with him, after convincing her to *sleep* with him . . . she was turning out to be a nutcase? It wasn't *fair*.

"I'm coming to get you!" she shouted. "I'm coming—"

"What do you think we should do?" Barney asked over the din. He sounded even more anxious than Trevor felt.

"I . . . uh, I think we should sedate her," Trevor stammered. "There's some—"

"Don't you come in here!" she screamed at the video camera. "Don't even *think* it!"

Trevor's jaw dropped. Her dark eyes seemed to bore into his own from behind the screen—as if she'd heard what he said. But that was impossible. She was in another building. He swallowed.

All right. Something has to be done. Immediately.

"I know what you're thinking, Trevor Collins," she snapped, her voice deeper than usual. "You're thinking: What's happened to poor Jezebel? Well, Jezebel is gone. And *I'm* here to take her place." She smiled, showing her teeth.

"Trevor?" Barney asked. His voice was urgent. "The sedatives?"

But Trevor was struck dumb. He could only shake his head and gape at the screen. Never had he heard anything so . . . *disturbing.* If this were a psychotic

132

outburst, it was unlike any he'd ever seen. And he'd seen *plenty*—what with all the COS kids. This was something far more virulent, far more powerful.

He almost believed her. The girl staring back at him *wasn't* Jezebel.

Who are you? he found himself wondering.

Jezebel's smile widened. "Don't worry, Trevor. You won't know who I am until it's much, much too late."

COUNTDOWN
to the
MILLENNIUM
Sweepstakes

$2,000 for the year 2000

5...4...3...2...1 MILLENNIUM MADNESS.
The clock is ticking ... enter now to
win the prize of the millennium!

1 GRAND PRIZE:
$2,000 for the year 2000!

2 SECOND PRIZES: $500

3 THIRD PRIZES: balloons, noisemakers,
and other party items (retail value $50)

Official Rules
COUNTDOWN
Consumer Sweepstakes

1. No purchase necessary. Enter by mailing the completed Official Entry Form or print out the official entry form from www.SimonSays.com/countdown or write your name, telephone number, address, and the name of the sweepstakes on a 3" x 5" card and mail it to: Simon & Schuster Children's Publishing Division, Marketing Department, Countdown Sweepstakes, 1230 Avenue of the Americas, New York, New York 10020. One entry per person. Sweepstakes begins November 9, 1998. Entries must be received by December 31, 1999. Not responsible for postage due, late, lost, stolen, damaged, incomplete, not delivered, mutilated, illegible, or misdirected entries, or for typographical errors in the entry form or rules. Entries are void if they are in whole or in part illegible, incomplete, or damaged. Enter as often as you wish, but each entry must be mailed separately.

2. All entries become the property of Simon & Schuster and will not be returned.

3. Winners will be selected at random from all eligible entries received in a drawing to be held on or about January 15, 2000. Winner will be notified by mail. Odds of winning depend on the number of eligible entries received.

4. One Grand Prize: $2,000 U.S. Two Second Prizes: $500 U.S. Three Third Prizes: balloons, noise makers, and other party items (approximate retail value $50 U.S.).

5. Sweepstakes is open to legal residents of U.S. and Canada (excluding Quebec). Winner must be 20 years old or younger as of December 31, 1999. Employees and immediate family

members of employees of Simon & Schuster, its parent, subsidiaries, divisions, and related companies and their respective agencies and agents are ineligible. Prizes will be awarded to the winner's parent or legal guardian if under 18.

6. One prize per person or household. Prizes are not transferable and may not be substituted except by sponsors, in event of prize unavailability, in which case a prize of equal or greater value will be awarded. All prizes will be awarded.

7. All expenses on receipt and use of prize, including federal, state, and local taxes, are the sole responsibility of the winners. Winners may be required to execute and return an Affidavit of Eligibility and Release and all other legal documents that the sweepstakes sponsor may require within 15 days of attempted notification or an alternate winner will be selected.

8. By accepting a prize, a winner grants to Simon & Schuster the right to use his/her name and likeness for any advertising, promotional, trade, or any other purpose without further compensation or permission, except where prohibited by law.

9. If the winner is a Canadian resident, then he/she will be required to answer a time-limited arithmetical skill-testing question administered by mail.

10. Simon & Schuster shall have no liability for any injury, loss, or damage of any kind, arising out of participation in this sweepstakes or the acceptance or use of a prize.

11. The winner's first name and home state or province will be posted on www.SimonSaysKids.com or the names of the winners may be obtained by sending a separate, stamped, self-addressed envelope to: Winner's List "Countdown Sweepstakes", Simon & Schuster Children's Marketing Department, 1230 Avenue of the Americas, New York, NY 10020.